THE CA

"Joseph!" Mary sh
Squinting in the r
at her, then followed he
riverbed. His eyes widened as he caught sight soldiers, who were now charging into the muddy channel after them.

Not wasting a moment, Joseph scooped Mary up in his arms and began running with her. (Or rather, ran as best he could considering the rain, mud, and treacherous ground conditions.) For a moment, he had attempted to maintain his hold on the donkey's reins, but quickly abandoned that effort – not because the beast was slowing him down but because the donkey, amazingly, was moving in the proper direction of its own accord.

Unsurprisingly, Joseph found his every step hindered by the mud. The suction of the muck was like a living thing, clawing desperately at his foot with every stride in an effort to make him stay in place, and only releasing him reluctantly with an audible plop as he continued moving forward. However, although his forward progress was understandably sluggish, it was undoubtedly faster than Mary could have moved on her own.

Risking a glance over his shoulder, he saw that – although also hampered by the mud – the soldiers were gaining on them. More importantly, comparing the forward progress of the legionaries to their own, it was clear that he and Mary would never make it to the other side of the river before their pursuers caught them.

THE CARPENTER

<u>Biblical Series</u>
The Carpenter

THE CARPENTER
A Retelling of the Story of Joseph of Nazareth

By

S.A. Wilson

THE CARPENTER

Copyright © 2019 by S.A. Wilson

Cover Design by Isikol

Edited by Faith Williams, The Atwater Group

This book is published by Panegyric Publishing.

ISBN: 978-1-937666-44-6

Printed in the U.S.A.

THE CARPENTER

ACKNOWLEDGMENTS

I would like to thank the following for their help with this book: GOD, first and foremost, without whom neither this book nor any other success I've had in life would be possible; and my family for always being supportive.

THE CARPENTER

Thank you for purchasing this book! If you enjoyed it, please feel free to leave a review on the site from which it was purchased.

Also, if you would like to be notified when I release new books, please subscribe to my mailing list via the following link: http://eepurl.com/gjAdw5

Finally, for those who may be interested, I have included my blog and Twitter info:

Blog: https://sawsatypicalblog.blogspot.com/

Twitter: @AuthorSAWilson

PROLOGUE

As he trudged along in the dark, his way lit by a lamp, Rabbi Aharon noted for the umpteenth time how little he cared for his current task. It put him squarely in the middle of an unprecedented and unsettling quarrel between two notable families in the region — two families which had, until very recently, expected to be united by marriage.

The betrothed were Mary and Joseph, children of their respective clan patriarchs. Joseph, a young man trained to be a craftsman and strong of body from his work with wood and stone, was noted as being pious and devout. Likewise, Mary had always been observed as being steadfast in adhering to the word of the Almighty. Thus, by all accounts, the union had seemed a sensible one, as the couple were both from respected families with good upbringings, not to mention comely of appearance. The expected wedding, however, had recently been stymied by an event that none had foreseen: after a visit with relatives in another town, Mary had returned pregnant.

Typically, the ensuing scandal and shame associated with such a revelation would be scathing, to say the least, but Mary — perhaps prodded by and at the insistence of her family — had latched onto a preposterous tale with the fervor of a zealot. She claimed that she had known no man and was still a virgin, but that an angel came to her and told her that she would nevertheless conceive and bear a child. Moreover, she told the story with such confidence and conviction that many were swayed to believe her. Needless to say, however, Joseph's family was not among those who found Mary's tale plausible.

All of this flitted through Rabbi Aharon's mind as he made his way to the house of Joseph's father, Jacob, who was understandably livid over the entire situation. As to Joseph himself,

1

rumor was circulating that he was contemplating the notion of quietly divorcing Mary as opposed to shaming her publicly. Although their betrothal a year earlier meant she was construed as his wife, no formal wedding had occurred and Joseph had not known her carnally, so he knew the child she carried was not his.

As to shaming Mary publicly, Rabbi Aharon wondered whether such was even possible. She was large with child; anyone who looked at her would immediately know her condition. Thus it would be quite surprising if there were more Joseph could do with respect to casting the shadow of shame Mary's way. Still, the issue of her conception had proven to be deeply disruptive and divisive, splitting the local Jewish community between those who supported Mary and those who supported Joseph. More to the point, it was that divisiveness which had led to Rabbi Aharon now making the trek to Jacob's house.

Basically, the threat of the pending wedding (or the cancellation thereof, depending on who one supported), had led to both families appealing to the local rabbis to offer advice and counsel on the situation. Mary was still willing to wed, which meant that the final decision as to whether such would occur rested with Joseph. His family, as expected, wanted the bridegroom advised to cancel the upcoming nuptials. Mary's family, on the other hand, wanted Joseph to be encouraged to take her as his wife.

Pressured as they were, the rabbis quickly decided that Aharon — the most junior among them — would have the honor of dealing with this task. At first he was excited at the prospect of offering advice in a tricky situation such as this. He quickly realized, however, that he was in an untenable position. No matter which way he counseled Joseph, there would be a well-respected family in the region expressing the opinion that he was a poor teacher and advisor.

Hoping that the dilemma would somehow resolve itself, he had put off speaking with Joseph until essentially the last moment

— the night before the wedding. (He had also been optimistic that his apparent dereliction of duty might cause another rabbi to be assigned this chore instead — perhaps Akiva, who was old and nearly blind. Enfeebled and burdened with declining health, the elderly Rabbi Akiva was unlikely to survive another winter, and would therefore suffer little reputational harm for the rendering of bad advice. Sadly, however, this obligation had stubbornly remained Aharon's to deal with.) Ergo, unable to procrastinate any longer, he had made his way through the dark and now found himself at Jacob's door.

He was quickly ushered into the house, which — like many of the neighboring homes — consisted primarily of numerous interconnected rooms surrounding a central, open-air courtyard. Joseph's family was very excited to see him. They had obviously been expecting him and concerned that he might not visit as requested.

After greeting the rabbi warmly, the family patriarch, Jacob, showed him to the courtyard and them directed him to one of the connecting rooms, where Joseph was doing some work. Rabbi Aharon thanked him and then asked for privacy as he approached the room in question.

As he walked, Aharon thought once more about the ways in which this dilemma could have been resolved. If only Mary had said she'd been attacked and assaulted! Then her situation would not be her fault. Or if her family simply said they'd changed their mind and given her in marriage to another. There seemed to be numerous ways out of this mess, if only—

Rabbi Aharon found his thoughts cut off as he noticed an odd light seeping out around the frame of the door to the room where Joseph was working. It was white like a cloud and intense — almost like lightning. Moreover, he thought he heard voices coming from inside, at least two. He leaned to the door and listened.

"—s the Almighty commands, and will guard him with my life," he heard Joseph say.

3

A moment later, the light faded. Then, before the rabbi could knock or announce himself, the door opened and Joseph came out.

His face had an odd but joyous expression, like he'd heard or seen something wonderful. In fact, it almost seemed to be glowing, and put Aharon in mind of a blind man who was suddenly able to see and take in the wonders of the world around him.

Joseph came straight to him. "Rabbi, I know that your counsel is valued and important, but I have received word from the Most High regarding what I must do. The Almighty directs my path."

With that, he turned and walked away into the night. Rabbi Aharon, still somewhat surprised, simply watched him depart without a word.

THE CARPENTER

Chapter 1

King Herod marched purposefully down the hallway of his palace, his agitation plainly evident on his face. Beside him was his close friend and advisor, Nicolaus, who struggled to keep up with his liege. Behind them were a half-dozen of the king's personal guard.

"Where are they?" Herod asked without breaking stride.

"The throne room, Highness," Nicolaus replied, "along with several additional guards." Herod cut his eyes at his advisor, causing Nicolaus to hastily add, "Just to prevent them from leaving."

Herod groaned slightly — a sound that Nicolaus found difficult to interpret, as it could have evidenced anything from mere contemplation to extreme displeasure (the latter of which was often accompanied by dire consequences). They walked in silence the rest of the way, and after a few turns found themselves at the rear entrance to the throne room.

Normally, only the king would enter through this door, as it opened to an area behind the throne where Herod normally sat during official functions. It was now early evening, and all official business had been concluded for the day. What currently required the king's attention was an informal matter, but one that had far-reaching repercussions.

Herod took a moment to concentrate, focusing on presenting an amiable disposition. Nicolaus stood quietly to the side, waiting. He knew that the king, despite being a harsh and severe ruler, could be exceptionally charming when the situation called for it. It was how Herod had won over Rome and gotten its leaders to appoint him as king. And now he needed to showcase a congenial personality in order to get something he desperately wanted: information.

Suddenly Herod smiled, his face beaming as if enraptured. It was a transformation that Nicolaus always found fascinating, but one which evidenced the king's guileful and crafty nature. Then, motioning that Nicolaus should follow, the king opened the door and went inside.

The chamber in which they now found themselves was rectangular in shape and, while not massive in size, was larger than most houses. Herod had initially wanted something more grandiose, but — upon the advice of Nicolaus — had eschewed the idea, as such lavish spending was likely to attract unwanted attention from Rome. Instead, the only concession to his ego was the throne itself; gilded, plush, and opulent, it sat on a dais and faced out towards the rest of the room.

Coming from behind the throne, Herod quickly took note of the fact that — aside from ten guards stationed at strategic points (including two on the floor at either end of the dais) — there were three men in the room. From their appearance as well as their attire, he recognized them as travelers from the East, quite possibly dignitaries. They were speaking together in hushed tones as he stepped forward, conversing animatedly in what he recognized as a foreign tongue. Their discussion came to an abrupt end as they became aware of Herod's presence.

"Greetings, friends," Herod said with a smile that didn't quite reach his eyes.

The three foreigners all bowed at the waist, almost in unison. A moment later, one of the trio, a tall fellow with an ebony complexion, stepped forward.

THE CARPENTER

"Salutations, great king," the man intoned, speaking with a slight accent. "Please allow me to make introductions. I am Balthasar, and my friends are Gaspar and Melchior."

His two companions each bowed their heads as they were introduced, which Herod acknowledged with a nod.

"Welcome," Herod announced. "Thank you for honoring my humble home with your presence."

"It is you who honor us, Majesty," Balthasar stated, "although we fear there has been some mistake."

"A mistake?" Herod repeated, then looked momentarily at Nicolaus, who suddenly appeared nervous. "Are you not the magi who sought the prophesied 'King of the Jews'?"

"We are indeed such," acknowledged Balthasar, whom Herod took to be the leader of the three. "But the mistake is not one of identity, Highness. It is, rather, a misunderstanding on our part as to the portents and signs we have observed."

A look of confusion settled on the king's face. "Would it be possible for you to elaborate?"

The leader glanced at his two companions, then said, "We have long been aware of a prophecy foretelling the birth of one who would be hailed the King of Kings. Our interpretation of the auspices and omens indicated that this was roughly the time of his birth, and because he was to be born in your kingdom, we assumed that he would be of your lineage. However, we have come to learn that none in your household are expecting or have recently given birth to a male child. Thus, it would appear that we have misread the signs."

THE CARPENTER

Herod rubbed his chin, appearing to reflect on his visitor's statement. "I, too, have heard this prophecy. It is said that this new king will be the light of the world — a Messiah — and I look forward to his coming. However, it would appear that my advisors and the learned men of my court have not been as diligent as you in foretelling the time of his arrival." The king looked pointedly at Nicolaus (who seemed to visibly wilt under the scrutiny) before turning back to this guests. "Nevertheless, I think that we may be able to help each other."

One of Balthasar's companions — the one called Melchior — made an odd sound that might have been a cough or a word.

"Lies!" Melchior said again in his native tongue, once more covering the utterance by combining it with a cough.

Ignoring his friend, Balthasar asked, "Many thanks, great king, but may I inquire as to the meaning behind your words?"

"It's simple," Herod explained. "You know the time of the Messiah's birth but not the location, while we know the place but not the time. I would suggest that we pool our resources."

Melchior made the bizarre coughing sound again, following which Balthasar noted, "It is a kind offer, great ruler, but we are not sure that we could make you a fair bargain. Our techniques require that we consult the augurs on a daily basis, and — as evidenced by the error that brought us before you — it is not an exact science. We could be off by days, months, or perhaps even years."

Herod nodded. "I understand. However, I still wish to share our knowledge with you."

The king motioned towards Nicolaus, who stepped forward.

"Bethlehem," the advisor declared. "This king you seek will be born in Bethlehem."

Balthasar turned to his companions, and the three of them excitedly began chattering in a foreign tongue. Not the most patient of men, Herod waited a few moments and then audibly cleared his throat. Much like his initial arrival in the throne room, the sound immediately brought the discussion among his visitors to a halt.

"Forgiveness, Majesty," Balthasar stressed. "We became excited at the news you provided and forgot ourselves."

"Not to worry," Herod assured him. "However, I would ask a favor of you."

"Of course, Highness."

"Once you locate this Messiah in Bethlehem, I would ask that you send me word. If he is to be the light of the world, as prophesied, then I would also come and show him reverence and worship him, too."

"We would be happy to do so, wise King Herod."

"Excellent," Herod said. "But tell me, how will you know him?"

"Pardon?" Balthasar muttered, surprised.

"How will you find this king-to-come? By what means will you identify him?"

Balthasar seemed taken aback by the question, but quickly recovered. "A good question, Highness. In all honesty—"

"Do not tell him about the star!" Melchior practically hissed in his own language. "We've been here but three days and have heard nothing of this king other than his despotic reign and wanton cruelty. He even killed his wife and several of his own sons."

"And we do not wish for three magi to be added to that list," Balthasar replied, forcing himself to smile. "You would be wise to hold your tongue, for this man is no fool. If you continue interjecting at inopportune moments, he will soon figure out that we all speak his language."

"Problem?" Herod asked, drawing Balthasar's attention.

"No, mighty king," Balthasar replied, shaking his head. "My companion Melchior considers himself the more senior of our group and chafes at the fact that he does not get to address you himself, as discourse with a king is a rare privilege. However, he is not versed in the language of this land, so the task — and the honor — falls to me. Melchior merely reminds me that he would have been a better choice as spokesperson."

Herod frowned in thought. "His words seemed more vehement than you would suggest."

"He chastised me fiercely," Balthasar offered, lowering his eyes, "for I failed to offer you any token of our esteem — a fact that I wish to remedy immediately."

From somewhere — presumably the folds of his garments — Balthasar produced a small wooden box. Herod raised an eyebrow in surprise. The man's hands had been empty a moment before, so the appearance of the box was unexpected. More importantly, it could easily have been a blade that he now wielded.

Balthasar took a step towards the dais, but immediately halted as the guards at either end suddenly drew their swords. Clearly they viewed either the box or

Balthasar's proximity to their king (or both) as a potential threat.

On his part, Herod was somewhat vexed. The guards should have searched the magi before bringing them into his presence. Although something as innocuous as a wooden box would probably not have been confiscated, Herod should have been made aware of anything significant they still carried on their persons. Then again, the visitors were magi; it was not beyond such men to have the means to spirit items into the room without detection. Nevertheless, Herod made a mental note to address the matter later as he motioned the guards to stand down.

Balthasar continued his approach and set the box on the edge of the dais before hastily stepping back.

Without a word, Nicolaus came forward and retrieved it. He could tell right away that it was well-made, the product of a master craftsman who had carved an intricate sunburst and other designs into the obviously-expensive wood. Lifting the lid, he saw that the box contained a jeweled ring resting on richly woven cloth. He quickly handed it to the king, who looked at it admiringly for a moment before turning back to the magi.

"My thanks for the honor you have shown me by this gift," Herod said. "Noting the hour, I will not delay you further."

Balthasar bowed his head in acknowledgment. "Thank you, Majesty."

"Before you leave, however, my question still lingers. How will you find this prophesied king?"

"As I was going to state before," Balthasar replied, "we do not have the exact means to do so. That said, we believe the omens will become clearer as the Messiah's birth draws nigh."

Herod drummed his fingers for a moment, thinking. He did not like the answer he had received, but there was little to be done about it. At the moment, at least…

"Understood," Herod finally said. "Thanks again for sharing your knowledge with me, and I would ask that you remember to honor your pledge and inform me when you locate the child."

"It will be done," Balthasar assured him, and with that, he and his friends hastily made their way out of the chamber, muttering excitedly amongst themselves in a foreign tongue.

Herod watched them leave, escorted by several of the guards who had been present in the throne room. As soon as the doors closed behind them, he turned to Nicolaus.

"Have them followed," Herod ordered. "I feel that they know far more than they shared with us."

"Consider it done," Nicolaus replied.

"Now, as to this king-to-come, why are my own advisors so ignorant of his pending birth?"

Nicolaus shrugged. "As the magi noted, the signs can be difficult to interpret. As our visitors themselves acknowledged, this might not be the true time of his arrival."

"Well, all my instincts say that those three are right. Now, we've known for several days that the magi were here and looking for this King of Kings. What have you been able to find out during that time?"

"We've queried the noble and highborn families of Bethlehem. Like your own household, none are expecting or have noted the birth of a male child who could fulfill the prophecy."

"The prophecy merely says that this child be *born* in Bethlehem, not that he be conceived there. What have you learned regarding other cities and towns?"

"As with Bethlehem, no family of note has a child or expectant mother who fits within the expected parameters."

"Hmmm," Herod mused, frowning in thought. "There has to be *some*thing. Some word or news of a birth of this magnitude."

"Well…" Nicolaus began, "there is something. But it's an oddity, nothing more."

"Tell me," Herod demanded.

"In Nazareth, there is apparently a young maiden who was betrothed but is now pregnant."

"Ha!" Herod barked in laughter. "Not the first time that's happened, and surely won't be the last."

"True," Nicolaus agreed, smiling, "but the girl swears that she has known no man. She insists that an angel visited her and told her that she would conceive of the Holy Spirit and bear a son."

Suddenly, the smile vanished from Herod's face. "A virgin birth? And nothing of that rings of prophecy to you, fool?"

"Majesty, you yourself just joked a moment ago about this girl's predicament. Her pregnancy is surely just evidence of her wanton ways, and her claims of carnal ignorance are nothing more than an attempt to avoid being stoned."

Herod merely grunted in response, clearly not convinced. The king obviously felt there was something about the story he'd just heard that warranted investigating.

"If I might make a suggestion?" Nicolaus offered after a few moments.

"Go ahead," Herod replied.

"You have Roman soldiers under your command — more specifically, a *centuria* stationed near Nazareth. Let us send a messenger bird ordering that they take this girl into custody and bring her to you."

"A *centuria* is a hundred men. It would be wasteful to have that number of soldiers solely to escort a pregnant woman."

Nicolaus bowed his head in obeisance. "I should have clarified, Highness. I meant only that a small number of them be sent to retrieve the girl. Perhaps a *contubernium*?"

Herod reflected on the suggestion for a moment. A *contubernium* was only ten men — eight legionaries and two auxiliary servants. While it was still probably overkill, it was far more reasonable than utilizing an entire *centuria* for the same purpose.

"Very well," Herod said with a nod. "Make it so."

THE CARPENTER

Chapter 2

"You are insane!" Jacob roared. "Your unbridled lust for this harlot has blinded you to common sense!"

"She is no harlot, and I am not a slave to any sinful desire," Joseph replied to his father. "The Almighty commands this."

"Quite clearly then the physician was wrong," Jacob stated. "Apparently you have *not* recovered from the head-kick our donkey gave you last month."

Rather than reply directly, Joseph merely stood there, staring defiantly at the family patriarch, which was unusual in itself. Ordinarily, Joseph was the most respectful of Jacob's children, obeying his father without question. On this particular occasion, however, they were stubbornly opposed.

They were currently in the courtyard of the family home. On the one side stood Jacob and three of his sons; on the other side was Joseph, dressed in his wedding garments.

Jacob was absolutely furious with his youngest son. Joseph's betrothed was, of course, the impregnated Mary, and today was to have been their wedding day. Once the strumpet's condition had become known, Jacob had, needless to say, cancelled the wedding and all related festivities. Moreover, he had gone to Mary's father and demanded the return of the dowry he had paid. (As an enticement, Jacob had dangled the idea of Joseph simply divorcing Mary rather than publicly proclaiming her an adulterer.)

Now, however, it seemed that Jacob's efforts had been undermined by his own kin. Joseph had seemingly gone out late the previous night, rousing friends and neighbors with news that the wedding would go forth as originally planned. Thus, Jacob had come out into the early light of day to find the wedding canopy set up and Joseph in his wedding attire. When questioned, Joseph had given honest answers as to his actions and intentions.

Jacob, understandably, was almost at his limit, frustrated and vexed by Joseph's inability to see reason in a situation where the appropriate outcome was blatantly obvious: the wedding could not proceed. Although weary of arguing, he was about to state his position once more when a servant, approaching from behind him, leaned forward and whispered in his ear.

Jacob's eyes widened in both anger and alarm. This was the final straw. He turned to the three sons who faced Joseph with him.

"Lock him up," he ordered, motioning at Joseph. "When you are done, meet me out front."

"Yes, Father," the three said, almost in unison, and then they converged on their younger brother.

****

Joseph fought valiantly, but in the end it was one against three. Thus — although he landed several solid blows — he was ultimately and unceremoniously tossed into one of the windowless rooms off the courtyard. The room in question was occasionally used to house animals, and was therefore capable of being barred from the outside (which is precisely what happened in this instance).

Ignoring his bruises, Joseph immediately began pounding on the door.

"Let me out!" he shouted. "Let me out! You subvert the will of GOD with your actions!"

Unsurprisingly, his brethren ignored him. Likewise, the servants in the house — knowing the will of their master Jacob — ignored his pleas and went about their business.

After a short time, Joseph ceased his yelling and efforts to beat down the door. It was clear that they would avail him little. Instead, he decided to do what had become habit with him when faced with a difficult problem: pray. Clasping his hands together, he closed his eyes and bowed his head, then beseeched the Father for help.

He was still making his supplication when, a short time later, he heard a noise outside the door that made him open his eyes. Recognizing the scraping of wood against wood, he realized that the outer bar was being lifted. His heart leapt a moment later when the door was opened and he saw his mother standing outside.

She gave him a gentle smile as Joseph hurriedly stepped out of the room and gave her a fierce hug. They separated a moment later, and his mother placed her hands on the sides of his face and looked deep into his eyes.

"I have heard many things about your betrothed — few of them good," she began. "However, you are the most faithful and devout of all my children, and if you say the Father has ordered you to wed this woman, then I believe you."

"He has, Mother," Joseph insisted, taking her hands in his own and kissing them. "It is His will that I take Mary as my wife and protect the child she carries."

His mother nodded. "Very well, then. Follow me."

With that, she turned and began walking towards the door that led out of the house.

"Wait," Joseph said softly, looking around warily as he fell into step beside his mother. "Where are my father and brothers?"

"A servant brought word that the bridal procession had left the house of Joachim and was en route," she replied. "Your father went to meet them."

"You mean warn them off," Joseph corrected, frowning.

Joachim was Mary's father. Under normal circumstances, Joseph would have appeared at her father's house with his friends and attendants to escort Mary — along with the rest of the wedding party — back to his own home, where the ceremony was to take place. Joseph, of course, had been held up by the argument with his father, and the bridal procession (or more likely, Joachim) had seemingly grown impatient with his tardiness and decided to start without him.

"I need to get to Mary," Joseph declared, imagining the scene that would occur when his father and brothers came upon the bridal procession. Harsh words would be exchanged, and possibly blows as well. In her condition, Mary didn't need to be anywhere in that vicinity.

"No need," his mother stated as they stepped through the outer door. She gestured towards the wedding canopy. Standing under it, Joseph saw Mary and several of her attendants, along with Rabbi Akiva. Excited, Joseph kissed his mother's cheek and then raced towards Mary.

As custom dictated, she was veiled, but Mary's eyes twinkled as Joseph approached.

"He's here, Rabbi," she announced excitedly as Joseph came abreast of her.

"Thank you for joining us, young Joseph," Akiva said. He didn't look directly in Joseph's direction, but seemed to stare off into the distance. This was not unusual, however, since Rabbi Akiva was generally considered to be blind at this point in his life.

"I apologize for being late," Joseph muttered. "Will you be officiating?"

"So it would seem," Akiva answered. "The other rabbis went with your father — presumably to forestall any potential violence."

Joseph nodded in understanding, but — knowing how his father felt about the current situation — he felt the other rabbis had undertaken an onerous task.

"Now," Rabbi Akiva continued, "I'm aware of the fact that much about this wedding is…*unorthodox*, shall we say. However, it's my understanding that you both wish to proceed with the ceremony. Nevertheless, I would hear it from your own lips."

"Yes, Rabbi," Mary said, and then turned to her betrothed. "Joseph, son of Jacob, I give you my oath that I have committed no sin and lain with no man. This child in my womb was begotten by the Holy Spirit, and it is an honor for me to carry him. However, the honor is not mine alone, for no ordinary man would be selected as the earthly father of this babe. Only one of great faith would be chosen by the Almighty for that role. Thus, it is not I alone who am honored to parent this child, but you as well. Finally, I give you my solemn vow that, if you will still have me, I will in all ways be the wife you so richly deserve and do all in my power to make you happy."

Joseph smiled at her. "Mary, daughter of Joachim, the Almighty has made His will known to me, and I therefore recognize and acknowledge the truth of this child's conception. Thus, I have no doubts about your virtue or chastity, and no qualms about taking you as my wife. Moreover, I will do all in my power to protect you and the child you carry, even at the risk of my own life."

As Joseph finished speaking, Rabbi Akiva nodded, as if pleased by what the couple had said.

"Very well," Akiva intoned. "Let us proceed with the wedding."

THE CARPENTER

INTERLUDE

The Horde watched from the shadows of a nearby house as the wedding ceremony between the man and woman proceeded. It glared menacingly at the couple, wanting to work its evil will upon them, but decided to bide its time until nightfall.

It was not a creature of flesh, so the sun did not harm it. However, it was never fully comfortable in the light of day, and therefore preferred to operate in the dark and gloom of night. Moreover, unless it desired to be seen, men usually remained ignorant of its presence, which was why none of those nearby were aware of it. How it came to be in this place, at this time, was almost happenstance.

As was its nature, the Horde had been going to and fro across the Earth, working what deviltry it could among mankind. Sometimes it merely whispered lies and half-truths, which was often all that was needed to corrupt the minds and souls of men. Also, despite being incorporeal, it had the ability to interact with the world around it, and was therefore capable of causing physical harm.

Finally, it had the ability to actually enter the bodies of living creatures and subvert them to its will. With respect to men, it typically targeted the feeble-minded or weak-spirited (although it helped if the person had a debased or immoral nature to begin with), and — after taking control of their bodies or gaining influence over their minds — often directed them to embrace wickedness and commit atrocities.

It was in the course of pursuing such abominable acts that the Horde recently sensed a power and presence that it immediately recognized: a seraphim. It was unusual for a member of the highest order of angels to descend to Earth, which meant that it was on business of great import. To the Horde, that meant an unparalleled opportunity to work mischief and it hastened to the spot where it perceived the heavenly being to be. The archangel, however, had already departed by the time the Horde arrived. The seraph's presence, however, had still lingered, having infused almost everything in the surrounding area, from plants to stones. More to the point, the indicated presence had also imbued a trail of sorts leading away from the area where the angel had appeared.

For some reason, the Horde had found the trail difficult to follow; it was as if some unknown power placed stumbling blocks in its path. Nevertheless, it eventually traced the trail to a pregnant woman — the same who was currently being wedded. In fact, the Horde had just found her the previous night and had contemplated attacking her then, but was dissuaded when it once again detected the presence of a seraphim. This time, however, it was the bridegroom that the archangel had visited, rather than the woman.

Although powerful in its own right, the Horde was not so foolish as to think it could challenge a seraphim. Thus it had stayed hidden, appropriately, in a mischief of mice until the heavenly visitor had departed, and remained there afterwards out of caution that the angelic being might return. It had not ventured out until the early light of day.

The Horde reflected on all this as it watched the marriage ceremony. Both the bride and groom had been visited not just by divine messengers, but by angels of the highest order. Based on that fact alone, the couple being wedded was obviously of great significance, although the Horde didn't understand how. That said, it didn't need to know all the details to recognize an opportunity — a chance to undermine the will of Heaven.

With that in mind, the Horde debated internally on how it might bring about the evil it now contemplated. Once evening came, it could whisper in the ear of the groom and see how susceptible he was to suggestion. (The Horde had previously been successful in getting a jealous groom to strangle his new bride on their wedding night.)

It could also take over some of the wedding guests and perhaps get them to murder the happy couple. In this regard, the Horde was different than others of its ilk. Whereas most of its contemporaries could only take over a single person at a time, the Horde was unique in that it could simultaneously enter the bodies of many. This was because the Horde, as its name implied, was a manifold being. It was a multitudinous entity — a swarm of imps, hellions, and other malignant spirits bound together in perverse fashion by unnatural laws and governed by a fractious and evil hive mind.

In the end, the Horde decided that the manner in which it disrupted heavenly plans didn't matter, only the end result. Then, smiling with malicious glee as the wedding ceremony ended and almost drooling in anticipation, it settled in to wait for nightfall.

THE CARPENTER

Chapter 3

As Joseph had foreseen, his father Jacob — accompanied by Joseph's brothers and others who felt he was in the right — had essentially gone to warn the wedding procession to turn back, as there would be no ceremony. Mary's father Joachim, walking with the wedding party, had steadfastly refused. Now the two men stood in the road, publicly hurling insults at each other.

"You are a scoundrel!" Joachim insisted. "We have a valid marriage contract between my daughter and your son, which you are brazenly trying to breach!"

"The contract assumed the bride would be chaste and a virgin!" Jacob countered. "Your morally degenerate daughter is nowhere near suitable, and you will not foist that shameless wench onto my household!"

Jacob did not seem to care that the bride was nearby, currently being carried in a covered litter, and could hear every word being said.

"Moreover," Jacob continued, "as your daughter's condition makes any agreement null and void, I again demand that you refund the dowry that was paid for her."

This triggered a new round of argument and insults, which the rabbis who were present failed to prevent (despite their best efforts). They had walked with Jacob from the anticipated wedding site at his house in hopes of keeping things civil between the two patriarchs, but were clearly not up to the task. Plainly speaking, emotions in this particular instance were simply riding too high for reason to prevail.

"We are not criminals," Joachim finally announced with pride. "We would not accept a dowry with no wedding in the offing."

"Oh?" Jacob muttered in surprise. "Then you agree to return what was paid?"

"I agree that the lack of a wedding would obligate the return of the dowry," Joachim explained.

Jacob frowned, finding Joachim's choice of words odd. The man seemed to be agreeing with him, but why would he suddenly change his mind?

Jacob glanced at the litter, where the bride still sat behind a screen of thinly-woven cloth. While it was easy to see that there was a person inside, it was impossible to make out who it was.

Suddenly suspicious, Jacob unexpectedly rushed towards the litter. He was not as young or as fast as he was in his youth, but he was still large and strong. To be precise, his action so surprised everyone that none moved to stop him — or even cry out — until he was at the litter. At that juncture, the shout from Joachim for someone to grab him was too late.

Jacob lifted the curtain and saw — to a certain extent — what he expected: a veiled young woman, seemingly ready for her wedding day. One glance at her flat stomach, however, made something abundantly clear:

The woman in the litter was not Mary.

THE CARPENTER

Chapter 4

"Husband," Mary said, "to where are we bound?"

"Bethlehem," Joseph replied. "It's where I was born. I have relatives there whom we can stay with until we have our own home. Bearing in mind how he feels about the child you carry, I don't think you would relish living under my father's roof or his constant scrutiny."

Mary nodded but didn't say anything. After most weddings, the bride and groom would retire to a bedchamber, following which bloody linen from the bed would be produced as proof of the bride's virginity. In the present instance, the end of the wedding ceremony had seen Joseph swiftly gather their belongings and some food, which he loaded onto a donkey. Afterwards, following a change of clothes, they had said a hasty goodbye to his mother and then departed.

They were now marching down a windswept road, leaving her hometown of Nazareth. Joseph walked at a pace that Mary found hurried but manageable, with her on his left and holding the reins of the donkey in his right hand. Their departure had been so swift that they were well under way before she had thought to ask her question about their destination. In truth, she had wondered whether she should even make the query.

Back when she and Joseph were first betrothed, her mother and wedded sisters had always advised Mary to be completely deferential to her husband after marriage — to always obey him and never question the things he said and did. Joseph, however, had never seemed to be that authoritarian. He had always impressed Mary as being the type of husband she'd be able to talk to, a man who'd share things with his wife.

As if in evidence of this, he turned to her unexpectedly and said, "I apologize. I should have spoken to you before regarding this journey, but in truth I only decided this morning that this was what we should do."

"It's fine," she assured him. "I know that everything you do is out of regard for me and this child. I was merely curious."

She reached out then and gave his hand a gentle squeeze — a sign of her trust and support.

Joseph smiled at the gesture, then asked, "Are you sure you wouldn't care to ride the donkey? It's generally well-mannered and docile, although it can become rambunctious if provoked."

Mary suddenly appeared curious. "Provoked how?"

"Well, my eldest brother smacked it on the nose last month, and it began kicking wildly. Even worse, I happened to be behind it at the time."

"Oh, no!" Mary squealed, placing a hand to her mouth.

"Oh, yes," Joseph said, then proceeded to tell her of the kick he'd received to head that caused him to spend several days in bed suffering from dizziness.

"In that case, I think I'd rather walk," Mary declared when he'd finished. "Plus, it feels better when I do — like it's good for the baby."

"Well, if you change your mind, let me know," Joseph stated. "This animal can carry a lot more."

Mary glanced at the items that currently comprised the donkey's burden. There was food for the journey, of course. There were also the few clothes they owned (other than what they wore), along with several household items, medicinals, keepsakes, and the like. The only other major item was a chest carrying the tools of Joseph's trade.

"Won't your father be angry that we've taken things from his house?" Mary asked.

"What things?" Joseph demanded. "The tools are mine. The donkey was a wedding gift from my mother's brother that I received when we were betrothed. The other items are our own and I paid my mother for the food. He has no claim on anything we carry."

Mary lowered her eyes and laid a hand on her bulging belly. "Do you think he'll ever accept me?"

"It doesn't matter if he does or doesn't," Joseph assured her. "*I* do."

Sensing his sincerity, Mary smiled and felt her heart grow lighter.

THE CARPENTER

Chapter 5

Jacob had raced back home to find — as he feared — that the wedding had taken place. Moreover, Joseph and that harlot Mary were now gone.

Thinking of his new daughter-in-law (the very notion of which made his stomach turn), Jacob couldn't help but reflect on the sham the girl's father had perpetrated. Knowing that Jacob would probably try to stop the wedding procession, Joachim had sent Mary on ahead by a different route, while having an imposter ride in the litter.

It was a bold and brazen gamble, and had paid off in that the wedding had indeed occurred. However, it in no way accounted for all contingencies. If nothing else, divorce was still an option. The trick now was getting Joseph to accept that it was the only acceptable outcome. In his current state of mind, however—

Jacob found his thoughts unexpectedly interrupted by a sound that was uncommon but familiar — and also alarming to a certain extent: the distinctive, rhythmic footfall of men marching in cadence, accompanied by the metallic clang of body armor.

Soldiers! Jacob thought. Ordering the rest of his family to stay indoors, he hurried outside in an effort to try to determine what this new development was.

As he stepped out of the house, Jacob saw that his ears had not deceived him: a small contingent of Roman legionaries stood right outside his home, having seemingly just come to a halt.

Jacob eyed the soldiers warily, noting that there were ten of them — a *contubernium*. That being the case, one of their number should be the leader of the group, better known as the decanus.

As if on cue, one of the soldiers stepped forward. From appearances, he struck Jacob as a grizzled veteran: approaching middle age, with some gray in an otherwise black beard, but still hale and well-muscled.

"I'm Atticus Canius," the man uttered in a gruff voice. "Decanus in the Roman army."

Jacob bowed his head slightly in deference. "Welcome to my home. In what way can I be of assistance?"

"You are Jacob?" the decanus asked.

"I am."

"We seek a woman known as Mary," Canius stated. "We initially sought her at her father's house, and our inquiries then led us here, where we were told she was to be married."

"You were not misled," Jacob said, "but she is not here."

The decanus eyed him suspiciously, then looked around. "I am somewhat familiar with Jewish weddings, and they are lengthy affairs, with days of celebration. If there were a wedding here today, it was unique in its brevity."

"My son married while I was absent and against my wishes," Jacob stated flatly. "The woman was with child, although she claimed to be a virgin."

Jacob noticed an odd look come across the face of Canius when he mentioned Mary's condition. It put him in mind of a wolf that had suddenly spied a lamb that had wandered away from the flock.

"And where are they now?" Canius asked, unable to mask his eagerness.

Loathe as he was to help Roman soldiers (even in regard to a strumpet like Mary), Jacob answered truthfully, saying, "Knowing I would not allow her under my roof, they promptly departed after the cercmony — I know not where."

Decanus Canius seemed to ponder this for a moment before responding. "You strike me as a prudent man — one who would realize the folly of misleading a soldier and representative of Rome."

Offended, Jacob drew himself up. "I have no reason to lie."

"Then you will not mind if we search your home."

Jacob bristled at the notion, but wisely kept a civil tongue in his head. "If it will set your minds at ease, you have my permission to do so."

"Your permission is not required," Canius informed him, then turned to the soldiers under his command. "Search the house."

THE CARPENTER

Chapter 6

Joseph briefly worried that he had made a poor decision.

He and Mary had left Nazareth for Bethlehem, but rather than traverse the most common and well-traveled route, he had chosen an alternate course. It would take them roughly the same amount of time, but — as it was a path not normally taken — it was less hospitable to travelers.

The logic behind his decision was simple: concern that his father would come after them. It would not take Jacob long to figure out that the wedding had taken place, and he would undoubtedly be livid. While not an exceptionally stern or overbearing father, Jacob did expect to be obeyed; Joseph's defiance would be galling, to say the least, and would likely spawn a response of some sort.

However, in her current condition, Joseph did not think it prudent to have Mary anywhere near an encounter that might escalate into a physical confrontation (as it had earlier when he'd found himself locked in a room). Thus, hoping to avoid any such conflict, they had departed from the main thoroughfare (and the company of others headed in the same direction) and were instead journeying to Bethlehem on a road less-traveled.

Joseph's concern at the moment, however, was more immediate. The path they walked was not well-trod like the main thoroughfare, and therefore the road was uneven in some spots, as well as overgrown with grass in others. The end result was that they had to be careful of their footing — especially Mary — which slowed their progress. That said, he did not think the decreased pace would add significantly to their trek in terms of time.

"Will it be dangerous?" Mary asked after Joseph explained the change in their itinerary.

Her husband shook his head. "Not particularly more so than the other road. The main issue is that — because fewer people take this path — there are not as many options in terms of food and shelter for travelers."

"What about bandits?"

Joseph shrugged. "There may be some, but not many. This being the less common path, there are few opportunities for highwaymen to waylay unwary travelers. They will have more success plying their trade on the main road where there are more people. Nevertheless, we'll want to remain vigilant."

Mary nodded, thinking her husband's words sounded wise. "And how often have you made the journey to Bethlehem on this path?"

"Once," Joseph admitted. "I was born in Bethlehem, and I've been there numerous times to visit relatives. However, my father wanted me and my brothers to be aware that there was another route we could take besides the primary roadway. It was a few years ago, but I remember the way."

Joseph spoke with an easy confidence that Mary found reassuring. Moreover, she found his tone to be pleasant and comforting. Encouraged by his willingness to engage in conversation, she continued to ask him questions (which he happily answered) about the journey that lay ahead.

THE CARPENTER

Atticus Canius was frustrated, but that was not an unusual state of mind for him. He was a man who felt constantly thwarted in life, both personally and professionally.

He was frustrated that — after over a decade of loyal service — he had only achieved the rank of decanus in the Roman army. He was frustrated that his family had never had the proper political connections to secure his future. He was frustrated that his wife never welcomed him home after a long campaign with open, loving arms like the wives of other soldiers did for their husbands.

The list went on and on. The catalog of issues that Canius found vexing could have filled the lengthiest of scrolls. So yes, frustration was a part of his daily existence, a dish served to him with mindboggling frequency. More to the point, this perceived torment and injustice had left him a cold, callous, and cruel individual.

The search of the Jew's home was just another item to add to the tally of disappointing outcomes. As the man had said, his son and new daughter-in-law were not on the premises. A more thorough search would likely have turned up *something* of value — jewels or gold most likely, as Jews were known to hide such items while feigning poverty. (That said, the household of Jacob did not appear to suffer from lack or hardship in any degree that the decanus noticed.) However, their orders were clear, and any delay would only make it that much more difficult to find their quarry. Therefore, he and his men had only probed to the extent necessary to verify that the girl was not present, rather than ransack the entire home.

Canius's frustration did not end there, however. After further inquiries, he learned that the newly wed couple had taken the road south leaving Nazareth. He had then pushed his men, marching double time, in hopes of catching them. (It also didn't hurt that other travelers — upon realizing that they shared the road with Roman soldiers — hurriedly got out of the way of the legionaries.)

Bearing in mind that the woman was heavy with child, it should have been easy. But, as with most things in his life, what should have been a simple, straightforward task somehow became rather complicated.

First, Canius came to the realization that something was amiss when, after marching for a period of time, they still had not come across the expected couple. At the pace that his *contubernium* was moving, he found it unlikely that a woman in the late stages of pregnancy could have moved quickly enough to still be ahead of them, and none of the travelers they had passed matched the description he had of Mary. That meant they had somehow missed the object of their quest.

Doubling back, the decanus began taking other travelers on the road to task, practically interrogating them about Joseph and Mary. Eventually he was made privy to the fact that the young couple had departed from the main road.

Cursing his luck, Canius had hurriedly led his men back to the spot where it appeared their quarry had detoured. Unfortunately, by that time, the last light of day was disappearing, and he did not fancy marching in the dark. From the state of the road, continuing their pursuit — even by torchlight — bore a certain amount of risk, and he did not fancy the thought of one of his soldiers getting a sprain or twisting an ankle, among other things.

Thus, feeling exasperated (and like a bit of a fool for all of the running around that he did), Canius called a halt to the day's activities and ordered his men to set up camp.

We'll catch them tomorrow, he thought, and then began to verbally lash his men for not getting a fire started (and carrying out their other duties) quickly enough.

On their part, the soldiers under Canius's command wisely held their tongues. They were well-aware of their leader's disposition, and knew that he was apt to take his frustration out on whoever or whatever was nearby when he was in this type of mood. Thus, each of them hoped that they would catch up to the woman and her husband the next day. (Although, bearing in mind the decanus's current temperament and the perceived affront to his dignity, someone was surely going to pay…)

THE CARPENTER

Chapter 8

Joseph awoke just after sunrise, but spent a brief moment being bewildered by his surroundings as he sat up: he was in a strange house, having apparently slept there on a mat in a corner. The sound of someone softly exhaling behind him drew his attention; turning, he saw a pregnant woman asleep on a mat next to his. And then it all came back to him.

The woman was his wife, Mary. Despite traveling at a deliberate pace, they had made good time the previous day, and — as Joseph had hoped — managed to reach a small hamlet that the road passed through before nightfall. The people there were friendly and hospitable, as Joseph knew from his previous journey through the region. One of the families had offered them shelter for the night. Wishing to show his gratitude, Joseph had pulled out the tools of his trade and performed a few repairs for their hosts (including leveling a table and fixing a wobbly chair) before retiring for the night.

All of this flitted through Joseph's mind as he stretched. Wanting to get an early start, he reached over and roused Mary by gently shaking her shoulder. She came awake almost at once, and — unlike her husband — seemed to immediately realize where she was.

"I apologize for waking you," he said, "but we need to get going."

Mary merely nodded in understanding as she sat up. A few moments later, they were both on their feet, eager to be on their way.

****

THE CARPENTER

It took little time for Mary and Joseph to get ready to depart. Before they did so, however, Joseph took a moment to once again thank their hosts — a man name Uri and his wife, Lirit — for their hospitality.

"Again, you have our gratitude," Joseph said. "It was kind of you to offer us shelter for the night."

"Think nothing of it," Uri said as he prepared to go into the fields and work for the day. "We could do no less — especially considering your wife's condition. Besides, you more than made up for it with your carpentry skills."

"Then I'm glad you consider it a fair exchange," Joseph stated.

"Fair?" echoed Lirit, holding an infant while a smaller child clung to her skirt. "It was a bargain from my perspective, considering my husband's complete inability to work with wood."

Her comment left everyone laughing. After a few moments, however, Uri composed himself and turned to Joseph.

"Don't take this as me rushing you out of my home," he said, "but I assumed you wanted to make an early start, so I had my eldest son feed your animal." He tilted his chin towards an older but solid wooden structure that served as a barn.

"Thank you," Joseph said sincerely. "You've been more than generous, and I hope our paths cross again in the future."

With that, he took Mary by the hand and began leading her to the barn. As they approached, his trained eye couldn't help but notice that the building could use a little work: the roof could stand to be repaired in a few spots, there was a crack in one of the walls (which seemed to be made of clay), and more. These were things he had noticed the previous evening when they had arrived and Uri had told him he could place their donkey in the barn. However, things that had not garnered much notice during twilight stood out much more starkly during the day. That said, the barn still appeared sturdy and could possibly go years before repairs became a necessity.

Upon reaching the barn entrance, they slipped inside and shut the door behind them. The interior was fairly dim, with the only light coming from a small window in one of the walls. As expected in an enclosed space used to house animals, the air was somewhat rank, but that was something both Mary and Joseph were accustomed to.

Looking around, Joseph immediately spied their donkey munching on hay in a small, wooden pen. Resting atop a small bench abutting a nearby wall were their belongings, including a box containing Joseph's tools. (He had brought the box out to the barn after making repairs the night before, so as not to clutter their hosts' home with too many of his and Mary's possessions.)

For a moment, Joseph contemplated checking everything, to make sure nothing was missing. He dismissed the notion a moment later, however; considering the kindness that Uri and Lirit had shown them, it seemed ungracious to suspect them of larceny. With that thought banished from his mind, he brought the donkey out of the pen and began loading their belongings on it. In almost no time, he had everything secured to its back. Turning to Mary, he was about to state that they were all set to go when a shriek of anguish rang out.

THE CARPENTER

He and Mary exchanged a worried glance, following which Joseph raced to the door of the barn. Suddenly cautious, he merely cracked it open and peeked out. Almost immediately, he realized the source of the wail he'd heard: Lirit, who was sobbing. At her feet was her husband, collapsed to his knees and looking dazed, with blood gushing from what looked like a broken nose.

In front of them stood two Roman soldiers, one of whom suddenly began speaking harshly to Lirit. Joseph couldn't make out what was being said, but from the man's tone, it was deathly serious. Hand visibly shaking, Lirit suddenly pointed towards the barn.

Alarmed, Joseph hastily shut the barn door and began looking for another way out.

THE CARPENTER

Chapter 9

Decanus Canius was feeling more than a little pleased with himself.

Able to grab only a few hours of fitful sleep the night before, he had made the fateful decision to get an early start on the day. Ergo, he had ordered his men to break camp well before dawn, and — despite his earlier misgivings about journeying by torchlight — continue their pursuit.

His soldiers had grumbled about the lack of adequate sleep but swiftly followed his commands. Accordingly, they were on the march in short order.

It had been just after dawn when they arrived at the hamlet — which Canius estimated to be home to no more than a dozen families. Noting that the locals were only just rising for the day, his decision to travel during the wee hours suddenly seemed prescient. It was unlikely that the couple they sought had made it farther than this location, so there was a strong likelihood that they had taken shelter within the hamlet and were still here. Splitting his unit into teams of two, they had then began to question the locals.

Canius had paired himself with a soldier named Tulio — a skilled swordsman, but far from the brightest of Rome's legions. However, he would usually do as ordered without question, which was what Canius had required at the moment.

The first house that the two of them had come to was little more than a hovel. A quick word with the widowed owner and a hasty search revealed that the couple they sought were not on the premises.

THE CARPENTER

The second house they approached yielded more succulent fruit. The owner there — a man named Uri — seemed evasive and shifty-eyed. To be specific, he struck Canius as being nervous. That wasn't an unusual sentiment when dealing with Roman soldiers, but something about the man made the decanus suspicious.

Going with his gut, Canius had given a surreptitious signal to Tulio, who had then punched Uri in the nose. Dazed, Uri had then collapsed to the ground while his wife shrieked. Knowing then that the legionaries were in no mood for games, she had immediately identified the barn as the place where they could find those they sought.

Wary of a trick, Canius had ordered Tulio to search the house while he himself would investigate the barn.

Thus, it was with a smug sense of satisfaction that he now approached the structure in question. Upon reaching the door, he was about to open it when he heard motion inside. Suddenly wary, he drew his gladius from its scabbard. As he pulled the sword free, it made a distinctive rasping noise as it rubbed against the metal of its sheathing. Weapon in hand, he then opened the door and stepped inside.

The interior of the barn was gloomy, but there was enough light coming in for him to see adequately. The first thing he noticed was a young man, obviously Jewish, scooping hay in the center of the floor with a pitchfork. Looking up as Canius entered, the young man stopped and merely stared at him.

"Who are you?" Canius demanded as he walked towards the young man.

"Rueben," the fellow replied.

"What are you doing here?" Canius asked, stopping far enough back to be out of reach of the pitchfork should Rueben decide to do something unexpected.

"My uncle asked me to clean the barn," Rueben replied.

"Your uncle?" the decanus repeated.

"Uri," Rueben explained. "I've lived with him and his family since my parents died."

Canius didn't answer; he merely stared at Rueben, then shifted his eyes to the pitchfork for a moment before turning his gaze again to the young Jew's face. Rueben, plainly understanding, released his grip on the pitchfork and let it fall to the ground.

Somewhat at ease now, Canius continued his interrogation. "I seek a man and woman — a couple. It's my understanding that they stayed with your uncle's family last night."

Rueben nodded. "I know of whom you speak."

"I was told that they were in this barn."

"They *were*," Rueben said, emphasizing the past tense. "They left shortly before you entered."

Canius frowned, once more starting to feel exasperated. He would now need to call his men together quickly and set out in pursuit.

He was about to turn and go when the sound of an animal neighing softly caught his attention. Glancing in the direction of the noise, he saw a donkey next to a pen not far from Rueben. He had been so focused on the young Jew before that he had not noticed it; now that he regarded it, however, he found himself looking the beast over closely.

There was nothing unusual about the animal in and of itself, but the decanus couldn't help but notice that the donkey had a full complement of articles tied onto its back. That implied that the beast was being readied for a journey of some length. (The only other option was that the poor animal had been housed in the barn all night fully burdened by the items it now carried, which struck Canius as unlikely.)

His suspicions aroused, the decanus turned back to Rueben, now giving the young man his full attention. Almost immediately, he spied something amiss: tucked into the cincture about the Jew's waist was a mallet — an unusual implement for a farmer to carry about on his person.

Stepping forward, Canius immediately brought up his sword, holding it at the young man's throat.

"Who are you?" he muttered angrily. "No lies this time, or I'll slit your throat."

The Jew gulped audibly, then said, "Joseph."

"And you hail from Nazareth?"

"Correct."

"Then you are the one I seek," Canius declared. "Where is your wife?"

"Hiding in the pen," Joseph answered, gesturing with his hand.

The decanus spared a quick glance in the direction indicated but didn't immediately see anything out of the ordinary. However, the interior of the pen was in an area that the light didn't fully reach. More importantly, he dared not take his eyes off the Jew for more than a moment.

"Woman!" the decanus shouted in the direction of the pen. "Get up, or witness your husband's lifeblood spilled."

"Please don't," said a feminine voice from the enclosure.

With his peripheral vision, Canius saw a form rise up in the animal enclosure.

"Come out," Canius commanded.

"I should help her," Joseph suggested. "She's due any day and cannot move swiftly."

"Stay where you are," the decanus ordered gruffly.

His sword still raised, Canius took a step back and then risked a glance at the woman. It was plainly evident that she was expecting, and he didn't doubt that her husband was telling the truth about her due date. As he watched, she gripped the front side of the pen as she slowly and methodically took a step towards the opening.

The decanus groaned in irritation; at the speed she was going, it felt like it would take the woman all day to exit the pen.

Canius turned his attention back to the woman's husband and pointed his sword directly at the man's face.

"Don't move," he said, and then stepped towards the opening of the pen to help the woman. A moment later, he went flying through the air as something like a thunderbolt struck him.

THE CARPENTER

Chapter 10

Joseph's plan had been constructed with haste and basically no preparation. After seeing the soldiers with Uri and Lirit (and observing the latter pointing at the barn), he had urged Mary to hide in the pen while he hurriedly pulled his mallet from the tools he'd loaded onto the donkey and tucked it into his cincture. (It wasn't as good as a sword, but — if needed as a weapon — it was an instrument he was familiar with.) He had then grabbed a pitchfork and began shuffling hay around with it in an effort to appear busy.

He had been slightly relieved when only one of the two soldiers had come through the door, but his comfort was short-lived as the soldier quickly saw through his ruse when he pretended to be someone else.

At that juncture, Joseph had thought all was lost. He didn't know why the soldiers were after him and Mary, but the fact that they sought the two of them at all did not bode well. However, he was given a small reprieve when the soldier moved to help Mary exit the pen. In doing so, the legionary walked directly behind Joseph's donkey.

Seeing an opportunity, Joseph had swiftly stretched out his arm and smacked the donkey on the nose — an action that he knew, from experience, would make the animal bray and kick wildly. He was not disappointed. The donkey's hind legs landed a powerful blow to the soldier's chest, sending him flying through the air. He struck the floor with a solid thud and lay there, dazed.

With the legionary incapacitated, Joseph tugged on the reins and spoke soothingly to the donkey, quickly calming it. He then turned to Mary.

"Hurry!" he urged in a soft but fervent tone. "We need to leave before he comes to his senses."

Mary nodded, glancing at the soldier who lay semi-conscious on the floor, moaning slightly. With the immediate danger gone, she now moved far more quickly in exiting the pen.

"Watch your step," Joseph warned, leaning down to pick up the pitchfork he'd dropped earlier (and which Mary had almost stepped on). Noting how spry she seemed, Joseph smiled. "You played your role well."

"I followed your lead," she replied. "When you mentioned that I could only move slowly, I took that as a hint and adjusted my pace, trying to buy you some time."

Joseph was about to respond when the door opened unexpectedly. And there, standing in the entrance, was the second soldier.

The legionary squinted, obviously needing a moment for his eyes to adjust. Recognizing that he had an advantage, Joseph suddenly charged at the man with the pitchfork leveled in front of him.

Suddenly, the soldier's eyes widened, indicating that he now saw the threat looming in front of him. He went to draw his sword, but it was too late, as Joseph was practically on him at that juncture.

However, rather than go for a killing strike (such as the face or neck), Joseph aimed for the man's sword arm. The tines of the pitchfork glanced off the vambrace covering the soldier's forearm, but caught the limb between them. With Joseph's momentum behind it, the pitchfork yanked the legionary off-balance before sinking deep into one of the clay walls, pinning the man's arm there. Not wasting a moment, Joseph — in one fluid motion — whipped his mallet from his cincture and then swung it at the soldier's chin (which was the area least protected by the legionary's helmet).

There was an audible crack as the mallet struck, snapping the man's head to the side. Arm still pinned, he slumped down to the floor, unconscious, but still breathing.

THE CARPENTER

Chapter 11

Neither Mary nor Joseph spoke for a while after leaving the hamlet. The soldier Joseph had struck with his mallet would live, but upon inspection appeared to have a broken jaw. Likewise, his companion would recover, having been protected from the full force of the donkey's kick in large part by his armor.

Joseph didn't care much for physical violence, but would fight when he had to (as he had demonstrated). However, it wasn't what had happened with the soldiers that caused the strained silence between him and his wife. It was what had happened afterwards.

Following his encounter with the second legionary, Joseph had quickly grabbed the reins of the donkey and left the barn, with Mary right on his heels. Seeing them, Lirit — still next to her injured husband — had cursed the two of them for bringing evil to her house, her family, and her town.

The two of them had tried to apologize, attempted to explain that they'd known nothing about the soldiers. Lirit, however, would have none of it; and so they had swiftly departed, with the woman's vilification ringing in their ears and feeling dejected because of what had happened.

But much to Mary's surprise, they did not continue on the road by which they had arrived in the hamlet. Instead, Joseph had led them through a nearby cornfield and onto a different path.

And thus they had traveled, in silence, since leaving Uri and Lirit. Although recognizing that her husband was deep in thought, Mary sought to draw him out by conversation.

"Husband, do we still journey to Bethlehem?" she asked.

"We do," he answered with a nod.

"But this is not the road we previously traveled," she stated.

"No," he acknowledged. "This is a more circuitous route."

"So it will take us longer."

"Yes, but I don't see many options," Joseph declared. "Those soldiers were looking for us specifically, which implies that they followed us from Nazareth. They'll be expecting us to continue on our prior path, so it's in our best interest to alter our course."

"But it appeared that they would be incapacitated for a while," Mary noted. "Won't that give us an adequate head start?"

Joseph shook his head. "No. The one who drew his sword on me wore the rank of decanus. That means he leads nine others. Assuming the one whose jaw I broke was part of his unit, there were eight other legionaries somewhere in the hamlet — presumably searching the other houses. There was a chance that at least some of them would follow us immediately."

Mary had to concede that her husband's logic appeared sound. Joseph, it seemed, wasn't just handsome of face and strong of body, but also sharp of mind. He would be a fitting husband for any woman, and Mary felt a slight twinge of sorrow that such a man — a godly man — would have his life burdened by her and the child she carried. And then she almost laughed at her own misgivings: the Almighty had chosen Joseph to be her husband precisely *because* of those qualities he possessed.

He was a man guided by faith, and in no way would view the task appointed to him by Heaven as onerous.

Turning her mind back to the issue of the soldiers, Mary asked, "Why do you think they were after us?"

"I don't know," Joseph answered with a sigh. "We've done no wrong, committed no crime. It's a mystery."

"Maybe—" Mary began and then stopped as she felt movement in her womb. She ceased walking as well, and instinctively put a hand on her stomach.

Joseph, noticing that his wife had fallen behind, stopped and turned.

"What is it?" he asked.

"The baby," she replied softly.

Alarmed, Joseph released the donkey's reins and raced to her.

"Are you hurt?" he asked, placing an arm around her in case she needed support. "In pain?"

"No," she replied, shaking her head. "It's the baby."

"Is it time?" Joseph blurted out, trying not to sound nervous.

"No," she assured him. "It's the baby."

Joseph gave her a confused look, clearly not understanding.

"It's the reason the soldiers are looking for us," she explained. "They're after the baby."

Chapter 12

They traveled until sundown, at which time they made camp near a small outcropping of rock at the base of a hill. Joseph quickly unloaded their belongings from the donkey and then gave the animal water. Afterwards, he tethered the donkey to a nearby bush, the leaves of which it promptly began to eat.

By this time, Mary had unpacked their own dinner, which was to be a simple meal of bread and cheese. However, before eating, Joseph had the presence of mind to start a fire, as it was likely to start getting chilly soon. It wasn't until he was convinced that the blaze was adequate (and likely to burn all night with little effort on his part) that he finally sat down and accepted food from Mary, who took a seat on the ground next to him.

They ate in silence for the most part, which was a continuation of how things had gone for most of the day. After Mary voiced her conclusion about the legionaries being after the child she carried, Joseph hadn't immediately responded. Instead, he had let the notion roll around in his brain for most of the afternoon. At the end of the day, however, he had come to the conclusion that Mary was probably right.

He took a moment to glance at his wife — more specifically, at her belly. There was no doubt that the child Mary carried was special. No one less than the Almighty Himself had plans for this unborn babe. That being the case, there were surely those who would — in attempt to undermine the will of the Lord — also seek the child. The thought made Joseph frown, as it meant that he had to take precautions and prepare for hazards he had not previously considered.

"Are you well, husband?" Mary asked.

"I'm fine," Joseph replied. "Why do you ask?"

"I'm sorry — it's just that you looked distressed."

"It is merely general concern regarding our journey," he stated. "Do not be overly bothered by it."

"You are my husband," Mary said. "If you are concerned, then I am as well."

"That's a kind sentiment," he noted. "Thank you."

"It's more than a sentiment," she declared. "We are wedded now, so we are one. Please don't be reticent about sharing your thoughts or feelings with me."

Joseph simply stared at her for a moment as he pondered her words. Mary was clearly perceptive and intuitive — traits that he found admirable. He had no doubt that she would be a fine mother and a devoted wife. More importantly, she had the ability to be not just support, but a source of strength for her husband — if he'd allow it.

"Very well," Joseph finally said, and then began to share his thoughts with her.

THE CARPENTER

INTERLUDE

The Horde was irritated.

Following the wedding of the young couple, it had waited until nightfall to pursue them, knowing that it could swiftly catch them wheresoever they went. However, as had happened previously, it had found the trail difficult to divine. Normally, the Horde encountered few hindrances when it sought to follow something or someone, but in this instance it found the proper path challenging to discern.

First of all, the couple's scent was obscured in some fashion. From the Horde's perspective, each human being had a unique smell, an odor which served as a spoor that could be tracked. But in this instance, the aromas associated with the couple were confusing. Rather than proceed in a specific direction, their scents seemed to bombard the Horde from all corners, coming from everywhere and nowhere simultaneously.

In addition, every person also had an aura — a unique reflection of their inner spirit that the Horde could perceive. In most instances, it was practically a beacon for the Horde, allowing it to pursue almost any quarry, day or night. Again, however, it found its efforts thwarted, as the couple's auras were muted in some fashion, making it not just problematic to distinguish them, but practically impossible.

In short, tracking the couple by its usual methods had proven onerous and galling for the Horde.

That said, the demonic creature had other dark gifts at its disposal. There were other means of locating its prey, and it had employed them. And, although not as straightforward as tracking quarry by scent or aura, these other tactics were ultimately just as effective, as proven by the fact that the Horde now had the couple in sight.

THE CARPENTER

The man and woman were currently settling in for the night. They had a fire going, and were engaged in conversation at the moment. Little did they know what horror lay in their immediate future, and the Horde felt exquisite delight as it contemplated the evil, heinous acts it was about to commit.

It had taken the Horde roughly a day to track the couple down, but now it would make them pay for the extra effort it had been required to exert. It would rip the baby from the mother's womb and squeeze the life out of it, then tear the woman limb from limb. And it would force the man to watch it all, helpless to prevent any of it, before killing him as well...

THE CARPENTER

Chapter 13

Joseph and Mary were talking, sharing their thoughts about the baby she carried and their common belief that it was extraordinary.

"With respect to this child," Joseph was saying, "I fully believe…"

He trailed off as an odd shift seemed to occur in the air around them. Without warning, a chill settled in, causing Mary to shiver involuntarily as their fire unexpectedly dwindled down almost to the embers. In addition, the night seemed to take on a deeper, more profound murkiness that had nothing to do with their diminished campfire.

Joseph rose swiftly to his feet, looking around warily. He was no stranger to abrupt changes in weather, but there was something different about what he and his wife were currently experiencing. There was an aberrant and unnatural quality to what was happening, and — as if further proof were needed — Joseph noted that the ambient noise had completely vanished.

Something's causing this, he surmised, but kept the thought to himself. His hair starting to stand on end, he looked around for the source of the corruption and dread that was pervading the air.

On her part, Mary was about to speak but was shushed by her husband before she could utter a word.

Pulling the mallet from the cincture (where he had kept it all day), Joseph continued scanning the area for —

There! he thought.

Not far away was a patch of darkness that appeared murkier…gloomier…than the surrounding night. Joseph leaned forward, peering intently. Nearby, the donkey began braying hysterically and struggled madly to get away from where it was tethered.

Joseph ignored the animal and kept his focus on the area in question. Much to his horror, he saw an oversized pair of eyes appear from nowhere. They blinked once, and then a large, dark form charged at them with a howl that seemed to shake the ground.

THE CARPENTER

Chapter 14

Acting on instinct, Joseph stepped protectively in front of Mary. Although their campfire had diminished greatly, there was still enough light for him to get a good view of the...*thing* that he had spied.

From his perspective, it was as if the night had taken on form and come alive, with an ebon, vaguely man-shaped figure rushing towards them. However, it was at least a head taller than anyone Joseph had ever seen, and the edges of the creature seemed fuzzy, as if its outer form were not truly defined. Its face was flat, with no nose — only the huge eyes he had previously observed and a ragged, gaping maw from which came a bloodcurdling shriek. Finally, it had misshapen, elongated arms that ended in bulky, wicked-looking claws.

All of this Joseph noted in the few moments it took the creature to cover the ground between them. Stopping in front of him and Mary, the creature reared up to its full height and howled again. Sensing an opportunity, Joseph threw his arm back and then swung the mallet with all his might...and went sprawling on the ground.

For a moment, Joseph was confused. The thing had been right in front of him — there was no way he could have missed. But somehow, the blow he'd attempted had connected with nothing. The creature had evaded him and now faced Mary, who was helpless.

Scrambling to his feet, Joseph — who was now behind their attacker — swung at the thing's back for all he was worth. His mallet passed through it as though nothing were there. With his strike meeting nothing where resistance had been expected, Joseph spun in a semi-circle, off-balance, but managed to stay on his feet. Dumbfounded, he merely stared at the thing for a moment, and then understanding dawned on him.

The creature didn't just look like the night; it was just as intangible. It was some type of shade, a specter, having form but no substance. Striking it was no more effective than punching the wind.

Suddenly the creature turned, and a moment later Joseph found himself gripped by one of its massive claws and hoisted off the ground. (Oddly enough, in the back of his mind, he noted that the creature could apparently be corporeal when it desired.) It pulled him in close to its face, and for a moment he feared it was going to bite his head off. Instead, it roared — a deafening, terrifying rumble that almost froze Joseph's blood in his veins as the thing's fetid breath blasted his face and hair like a winter wind.

More horrid, however, than the sound it made was what Joseph saw when it pulled him near. The creature's hide (if it could be called such) was worlds apart from anything he had ever seen. Unlike the skin of a man or the pelt of a beast, its tegument appeared to be composed of living beings. There was a host of impish, fiendish faces, along with twisted and perverted forms, all bound together in some unholy fashion into a single frame. Even when it roared, the inside of its maw revealed the same revolting amalgam of unearthly visages and shapes.

But before the truth of what he was seeing could settle into Joseph's mind, he found himself slammed into the outcropping of rock that they had made their camp near. The force of the impact rattled his bones and made him see stars for a moment. The creature released him, and he slid to the ground, stunned. As he watched, it turned towards Mary, whose eyes were bulging in fright.

Joseph struggled to move, but his body refused to obey him. Considering how hard he had been thrown against the rock, it was no surprise that he had trouble coordinating movement. In fact, he was battling just to stay conscious.

And so — aside from sending a brief prayer to the Heavenly Father — all he could do was watch in horror as the specter drew back a clawed hand and swiped mercilessly at Mary's belly.

THE CARPENTER

INTERLUDE

PAIN!!!

Shrieking in agony, the Horde fled into the night, leaving the couple behind at their campsite. It felt as though every part of its being had been ripped to shreds and set aflame. Never in its existence had it known such torment.

As it ran, heedless of direction or anything in its path, the Horde sought to understand what had happened.

It had subdued the man easily enough. Although he had tried to attack the Horde, his efforts had been futile and he had ended up slumped on the ground, barely conscious. The Horde had then clawed at the woman's belly, intending to rip the unborn babe out of her. And that's when it happened.

That's when — at the moment its claw touched the woman — the searing agony had gone coursing through the Horde, torrid and blistering like the fires of Gehenna.

And with that thought came understanding. It was the child.

The child was the reason that the Horde had trouble finding the auras of the man and woman.

The child was the reason it had been unable to pick up their scent.

The child was the reason two seraphim had descended to the earthly plane.

The child was the centerpiece of it all. The child was the key. The babe was nonpareil — pure and perfect in a way that defied explanation or understanding, not just in body but also in spirit. More to the point, the child was beyond the Horde's ability to harm (and, as had just been proven, there were dire repercussions for attempting to do so).

Still smarting from the injury it had suffered, the Horde began to feel a growing, seething hatred for the baby the woman carried. Not only had it suffered excruciating pain because of the child, but it had been thwarted in its desire to frustrate the will of Heaven, and it was the latter of these that it found most offensive.

Growing ever more angry, the Horde made a fateful decision: it would destroy this child — even at the cost of its own existence. But it was a statement easier said than done, since it could not harm the child directly. However, it could certainly do so indirectly — *through the body of another. Moreover, although its attack on the woman had been an abysmal failure, there had been another unexpected outcome: physical contact had enhanced the Horde's perception of its intended victim and the child she carried. In brief, it could track them now.*

Having decided on a course of action, the Horde reached out with its senses, seeking someone or something through which it could act against the couple it had attacked — and more specifically, the unborn child the woman carried. Ideally, it would prefer an individual who already had a grudge against the man and woman; it would be easier to guide the actions of such a person.

Much to its surprise, the Horde found not just one such person but nine of them. Swiftly, it headed towards those it had identified, all the while thinking of how wonderful it would be when it finally took the life-breath from the child that had injured it.

THE CARPENTER

Chapter 15

Canius, as usual, was frustrated. At the moment, he sat on the ground — along with several of his men — around their campfire. Not wanting to appear weak, he struggled to keep his breathing slow and even. Truth be told, however, he ached all over.

The kick he had received from the Jew's donkey had been the equivalent of getting struck with a battle mace. Fortunately, his armor had absorbed most of the blow, but it had not been a painless experience. Not only had he struck his head when he hit the floor (which had left him semi-conscious), but the rest of his body had apparently landed hard and awkwardly. Fortunately, nothing was broken, but his neck hurt whenever he turned it to either side, his left leg felt like it was being jabbed with needles whenever he walked, the wrist on his sword arm was swollen, and his chest — where the animal's kick had landed — ached with every breath he took.

There was an assortment of other bumps and bruises, but those were the main things. However, it was important to the decanus not to appear frail in front of his men. It was bad enough that they had come upon him still on the floor of the barn, unable to rise.

The closest thing that the hamlet had to a physician was an old midwife, and she had been fetched right away. She had treated him as best she could and suggested a day of rest, but Canius had spurned her advice. Not only would it send the wrong message to his men, but it would delay them in pursuing the couple.

Of course, the decanus had fared better than the soldier he had paired himself with, Tulio. The man had suffered a broken jaw, but more importantly, Tulio — who had never been very bright to begin with — seemed to have finally received one blow too many to the head. Basically, while he regained consciousness, Tulio did not seem to fully regain his mental faculties and was in no condition to even care for himself, let alone travel.

By Canius's estimation, his own treatment and recovery time had cost them at least half a day. At that juncture, he had decided to leave Tulio, with strong words to the people of the hamlet that he was to be properly cared for. In fact, Tulio's presence was the only reason he did not order his men to burn every house to the ground, as it was death to strike a Roman soldier on official business. (Even though it was the man Joseph who had caused his and Tulio's injuries, Canius felt the entire community should be reprimanded for having sheltered the man and his wife for the night.) Thus, after capturing their quarry, the decanus planned to return along the same route to retrieve the injured soldier, at which time he would mete out an appropriate sanction.

Canius yawned — normally an innocuous act, but this time it was accompanied by aches and pains. He was exhausted, and it clearly showed. Despite wanting to keep up a façade of strength for his men, his weariness had been plainly evident — from his inability to maintain even a slow pace to his decision to make camp well before twilight.

In short, he was slowing the entire unit down, which would make it even more difficult to catch up to the couple they sought. He briefly pondered sending his men ahead, but felt that they would get the glory if — no, *when* — the mission ended successfully. He would simply have to ignore the pain and push himself onward by sheer will, if necessary.

The decanus yawned again, feeling that he could no longer keep sleep at bay. Still reflecting on all that had occurred — and planning on how to proceed on the morrow — he started to doze. However, just before his eyes closed, he saw an odd sight: the darkness around them seemed to coalesce into a hulking, shadowy form that strode brazenly into the middle of their camp...

THE CARPENTER

Chapter 16

Neither Joseph nor Mary slept well. The attack by the fiendish specter had unsettled them both, to say the least. Thankfully, it had fled into the night, with the only remnant of its presence being a foul and pungent malodor that even a stiff breeze could not fully remove.

After the creature vanished, it had taken a few moments before Joseph — with Mary's help — was able to rise to his feet. At that juncture, although no longer comfortable with his initial choice of a campsite, he had to decide whether to brave the dark (and whatever else might be lurking in it) or stay put. In the end, he felt that Mary and her baby would be safer elsewhere. Decision made, they had quickly packed up and moved to another location.

It had been slow going in the dark, with only a candle for illumination, but they had eventually found a small clearing that Joseph felt would serve their purposes. There they made camp for the second time, but — despite not being disturbed during the night — both found peaceful slumber evasive.

The next morning saw them rising with the dawn and preparing to continue their journey. However, having altered their route several times to avoid familial conflict, Roman soldiers, and now a demonic fiend, they were well off the beaten path. That said, Joseph knew the general direction of their destination.

"We're not lost," he assured Mary as they began walking along a path that could best be described as a trail. "We're headed in the right direction, but we're not traveling a route that I know."

"Will it add greatly to our sojourn?" his wife asked.

"A day, perhaps. Maybe two, if we move at a moderate pace."

Mary nodded, recognizing in her husband's response a concession to her: he was willing to travel at a slower speed if such were more comfortable for her.

"Do not let concern for me impede our progress," she stated. "The Almighty shall maintain my strength."

"I do not doubt it," Joseph conceded. "And after last night's encounter, I would prefer to arrive in Bethlehem as soon as possible."

"Speaking of last night, I failed to say it earlier, but I thought you were very brave," Mary said, giving him an admiring look.

"No more than you," her husband admitted. "There are few women who could have stood their ground before that thing."

"I stood my ground because I was frozen with fear," she said with a giggle.

Joseph found her laugh infectious, and a moment later he was chuckling as well.

"Apparently your fear comes across as courage," he said, "because you chased our assailant off."

"I'd be happy to take credit," she replied, suddenly sounding somber, "but I think we both know what really happened."

Joseph gave her a deliberate nod. "The baby."

This was the first time they had talked about what had happened, acknowledged what had truly occurred. Somehow, the child in Mary's womb had run the creature off, and once again, Joseph found himself marveling at the nature of the baby his wife carried. It was far more precious and unique than he had ever realized, and he felt humbled that he had a role to play in its life.

****

Following their brief discussion, Mary and Joseph traveled in relative silence for a while. Mary was happy to note, however, that the lull in conversation was neither awkward nor uncomfortable. They both simply seemed to be lost in their own thoughts.

Joseph in particular was deeply contemplative, but not for the reasons Mary may have thought. The day was overcast, and off in the not-too-distant north he could see dark storm clouds, accompanied by lightning and the occasional rumble of thunder. From all indications, there was a tempest brewing, and it looked like it might be headed in their direction. Joseph didn't like the idea of Mary getting caught in the rain and perhaps catching a chill, so he was determined to find shelter before that happened.

Around noon, the trail that they were on broadened, and they found themselves facing a wide expanse of open ground that stretched out to either side as far as the eye could see. The ground itself seemed cracked and desiccated, putting Mary in mind of an earthen pot that had split into pieces after being dropped.

"What is this place?" she inquired.

"Dried riverbed," Joseph answered.

"What happened to the water?"

"Evaporated," he explained. "It'll come back when the rains return."

THE CARPENTER

As if on cue, a light drizzle suddenly began to fall. It was bad timing, but the weather had held up until that point, so Joseph supposed that he should be grateful.

"Come on," he said, taking Mary firmly but gently by the elbow while leading the donkey with his other hand. "We need to hurry."

Joseph tried to stress urgency without making Mary unduly alarmed, but the truth was that he was now worried about more than his wife just catching a chill. He had an idea of where they were, and it was his understanding that the area was prone to flash floods. With rain now coming down, it was imperative that they cross the riverbed quickly.

Faster than Joseph would have thought possible, the cracked ground became muddy, and their progress was slowed tremendously as their feet began sinking up to their ankles in muck.

"What's that?" Mary asked.

Joseph, who had been looking down to stay cognizant of their footing, glanced up and then followed Mary's gaze. The rain was coming down harder now so he had to squint in order to see through it, but after a moment he picked out the object that had aroused Mary's curiosity: a sizeable panel of wood — big enough for a score of people to stand on — lying in the middle of the riverbed directly ahead of them. It was square-shaped, with a railing of some sort on two sides. There was also a length of rope that lay coiled around one of the rails.

"Looks like a ferry," he said after a moment. "It was used to take people from one side of the river to the other — before it dried up, of course."

Mary nodded and was about to say something when she thought she heard voices. Looking back the way they had come, she was certain that she saw movement — people — back at the point where the trail met the river.

Holding a hand up to her forehead in order to shield her eyes, she peered again and saw that she was right. There *were* people there.

A moment later, she drew in a harsh breath as she became aware of something else about the new arrivals: they weren't just people — they were soldiers.

Roman soldiers.

Legionaries.

THE CARPENTER

Chapter 17

Canius had awakened feeling different. He had fallen asleep burdened by frustration and exhaustion, but had arisen refreshed and reinvigorated. Even more, he felt energized — more alive than he had in years.

If that weren't enough, he also felt a renewed bond with his men (or rather, the eight of his men still with him). In a unit such as theirs, soldiers generally grew close and often regarded each other as family. That had happened with his legionaries, but lately the relationship had felt strained. His men were still loyal and obedient, but recently there seemed to be more grumbling than usual, a growing current of dissatisfaction and discontent. That was gone now, having seemingly evaporated like dew under the light of a summer sun.

Canius couldn't fully explain it — any of it — but the decanus attributed the change in himself (and his men) to the dream.

****

He could only remember bits and pieces of what he'd dreamt (and even those parts were hazy), but when he concentrated, Canius could recall vague images of a dark form entering their camp. No, not just entering the camp, but entering *them* — him and his men. At the same time, he had sensed a shared desire with the form, a common objective.

Whether it was the dream or something else, the decanus now found himself obsessed with a singular purpose: to find the couple they sought, and punish them — especially the unborn baby.

THE CARPENTER

Truth be told, he had never given much thought to the child before. Frankly speaking, it had initially been merely a means to help identify the woman they sought. But something about the child now sparked outrage in him, fury and indignation on a scale he'd not previously felt.

And so they had broken camp and started out early, much like the prior morn. However, unlike the end of the previous day, they made excellent time, practically running the entire morning. Most surprising to Canius was the fact that he himself — previously the weak link in the chain with respect to marching at a decent clip — was able to keep up without effort. It was as though he and his men were now tireless, filled with an infinite amount of vigor.

The odd thing was that his aches and pains from the previous day were still there, but they no longer bothered him. Some part of him had shut away the pain, cut it off from the rest of his being.

As to the route they traveled, some inner compass pointed the way they should go. Again, Canius could not explain it, but he and his men knew unerringly the proper direction.

Thus they had journeyed, guided by what seemed to be instinct. Somehow, however, their actions bore fruit, as the path they had been traveling all day abruptly widened as it met a dried riverbed.

And there, attempting to cross as rain began coming down heavily, was their quarry.

Chapter 18

"Joseph!" Mary shouted anxiously.

Squinting in the rain, her husband turned to look at her, then followed her gaze back to the edge of the riverbed. His eyes widened as he caught sight of the soldiers, who were now charging into the muddy channel after them.

Not wasting a moment, Joseph scooped Mary up in his arms and began running with her. (Or rather, ran as best he could considering the rain, mud, and treacherous ground conditions.) For a moment, he had attempted to maintain his hold on the donkey's reins, but quickly abandoned that effort — not because the beast was slowing him down but because the donkey, amazingly, was moving in the proper direction of its own accord.

Unsurprisingly, Joseph found his every step hindered by the mud. The suction of the muck was like a living thing, clawing desperately at his foot with every stride in an effort to make him stay in place, and only releasing him reluctantly with an audible plop as he continued moving forward. However, although his forward progress was understandably sluggish, it was undoubtedly faster than Mary could have moved on her own.

Risking a glance over his shoulder, he saw that — although also hampered by the mud — the soldiers were gaining on them. More importantly, comparing the forward progress of the legionaries to their own, it was clear that he and Mary would never make it to the other side of the river before their pursuers caught them.

With that understanding, Joseph changed tactics. Escape wasn't possible, but they could make a stand. And so, rather than the opposite shore, he made the ferry their destination. He honestly didn't think he could defeat a unit of armed, trained soldiers all alone, but facing them was preferable to being cut down from behind. Also, he had the Almighty on his side…

Just before reaching the ferry (which, in truth, was little more than a raft), Joseph took another look back. As he did, he saw one of the lead soldiers lose his footing and go sprawling in the mud. Even better, most of his fellow legionaries tripped over him (or another of their fellows) such that all but one of them ended up down in the mud. Joseph sent up a silent prayer of thanks to the Heavenly Father and continued plodding forward.

Once he reached the raft, Joseph quickly put Mary on board. There was railing on the side they had approached and she had to duck underneath it (which could have been challenging, given her condition), but she managed to do so fairly easily with her husband's help. Turning to him, a look of utter anxiety suddenly settled on her face.

"Joseph!" she shouted. "Behind you!"

Her husband spun around. Only a few feet away from him was one of the soldiers — the only one who'd managed to stay on his feet when his comrades fell. The legionary had his sword in hand, raised high, and was bringing it down in a striking motion.

Joseph ducked — more of a reflex than an intentional act.

As a result, rather than splitting his intended victim's skull open, the soldier's sword bit deep into the wood of the railing.

At that juncture, Joseph noticed three things. First and foremost were the legionary's eyes: they were completely black, with no white whatsoever. It gave the man a frightening and unholy appearance.

Next, there was a biting, rancid odor that accompanied the soldier. Although it stung his nose, there was something eerily familiar about it (although Joseph couldn't immediately place it).

The final thing that he became aware of was that the soldier's sword was seemingly stuck in the railing, as the man grunted with effort, trying to pull it out.

Sensing an opportunity, Joseph stepped forward and shoved the legionary in the chest as hard as he could. The force of his push seemingly helped the soldier yank his sword free; however, the man went stumbling back for a few paces before completely losing his footing and falling down backwards.

The soldier lay there for a moment, and then started groaning loudly. Joseph's eyebrows rose in surprise; he had given the man a hard shove, but — considering his armor — not nearly forceful enough to have caused much harm, if any. And then he understood: the legionary wasn't groaning in pain. He was groaning with the effort of trying to rise.

In short, just as it had pulled at Joseph's feet, the suction of the mud had gotten a stout grip on the soldier after he fell. Coupled with the weight of his armor, the man was seemingly unable to rise (although he was visibly straining with the effort). Now Joseph understood why the other soldiers may have been so slow to continue the pursuit. As he looked, however, he saw that most of them were just getting to their feet again — although one of them was already up and heading in his and Mary's direction.

THE CARPENTER

A terrified neighing brought Joseph back to himself. Just a few feet away was their donkey, which — with eyes bulging — was giving a wide berth to the fallen legionary. Racing over to it, Joseph grabbed the reins and began half-dragging it to a side of the raft that was bereft of railing. Scrambling aboard, he began hauling on the reins, trying to pull the donkey on board by sheer force (despite how uncomfortable it probably was for the animal). A moment later, Mary rushed over to join him, getting a grip on the straps and adding her strength to his, as their pack animal seemed to be stuck in the mud.

As they pulled, Joseph turned his gaze in the direction of their pursuers. The soldier he had knocked down was still stuck in the mud. However, one of his fellows was about halfway to the raft. The rest were only just starting to head their way.

Fearful of the odds against them, Joseph looked to the sky and muttered, "Father, help us."

As if in response, a sound like the roar of a thousand lions suddenly shook not only the ground but seemingly the very air around them. Joseph turned to look up-river — the direction the sound had come from — and marveled at what he saw: a giant white wall, three times the height of a man, rushing at them faster than the speediest chariot.

Flash flood, he immediately realized, recognizing the "white wall" as froth from a destructive, tidal wave of water.

"Mary!" he screamed, even though his wife was right next to him. "The rope!"

Not knowing if she could hear him over the thunderous boom of rushing water, he pointed for emphasis at the rope he'd noticed earlier. Mary nodded to show she understood and then dashed to where it was located and began uncoiling it from the railing.

Their donkey, braying madly in fright, unexpectedly found an inner reserve of strength and — after getting its forelegs on the raft — heaved itself aboard. As he began tying the animal's reins to the railing, Joseph spared a moment to look at their pursuers again.

The soldier who had fallen backwards in the mud was still in the same position. Most of the others, having noticed the oncoming floodwaters, had begun hastily scrambling back to shore. (Apparently they realized that their armor put them at significant risk of drowning.) One of their number, however, stood frozen in a position that was about midway between the raft and the shore, his head swiveling back and forth between the riverbank, the oncoming water, and the ferry.

Joseph immediately understood the man's dilemma. The poor fellow was unable to decide which direction offered him the greater chance of safety. Seemingly throwing caution to the wind, the soldier began running towards the raft.

By that time, Joseph had joined Mary and was busy with the rope. Thankfully, the cord was lengthy by virtue of having been used to pull the ferry back and forth across the river. Working as fast as possible, he made sure one end of it was securely tied to the railing before looping a coil of it around Mary, tying it (for obvious reasons) above her belly but below her bosom. He then tethered it to himself around the waist before knotting the other end of it to the railing once again.

By the time Joseph finished with the rope, the water was practically on top of them — a towering wave that seemed every bit as daunting as the Great Deluge faced by Noah.

"Hold on!" he shouted to his wife. Following his instruction, Mary gripped the railing with both hands, clutching it tightly in white-knuckled trepidation.

Joseph took one last look in the direction they'd come from and, much to his surprise, saw that one of the legionaries was almost at the raft. It was the soldier who had been at the midway point — the one who had hesitated with respect to which way to run for safety. However, the man had barely placed a hand upon the railing, obviously preparing to pull himself aboard, when the water struck. With a wail of anguish, the soldier was knocked away and carried off, like a blade of grass swept up and buffeted by the wind.

And then Joseph had no more time to dwell on the soldier's fate, as he suddenly found himself not only pounded by the water, but completely submerged.

THE CARPENTER

Chapter 19

The minutes following the arrival of the floodwaters were among the most terrifying of Joseph's life. When the wave hit, he had tried to shield Mary with his body, draping himself over her protectively, with an arm around her while gripping the railing with his other hand.

The water had struck like a battering ram, half knocking the wind out of him while unexpectedly seizing the raft and shoving it along with a jolt that knocked both Mary and Joseph's feet out from under them. At the same time, they lost their respective grips and went tumbling up and over the side as the raft shot beneath them. His eyes open, Joseph lunged desperately for the railing, only to have it brush his fingers tantalizingly before moving out of reach. He and Mary thereby found themselves floating underwater.

In truth, however, it was less like floating and more akin to being a hooked fish that a fisherman was dragging in. After being shaken free of the railing, the only thing that had kept the young couple from being washed away was the rope Joseph had used to tie them to the raft. Unfortunately, being bound to it meant they were now dragged along with it, perforce, by the rushing water.

His lungs starting to burn, Joseph noticed something that both frightened him and gave him hope: the raft — although pushed along by the water — was starting to rise. It was still buoyant.

That was good news — *if* they could reboard. On the other hand, if they couldn't, Joseph feared for their chances of survival; being dragged behind (and possibly beneath) the raft was sure to be a death sentence. (It also didn't help that the water, aside from being murky, was also full of dangerous objects and debris — like an uprooted tree that went streaking by them, barely missing Mary's head.)

Almost frantically, Joseph grabbed the rope still tethering him to the railing. Praying for strength, he began pulling himself hand-over-hand towards the raft, drawing Mary in behind him.

He fought the temptation to check on his wife. Like himself, she had to be fiercely battling the urge to breathe, but there was nothing he could do for her if she were in trouble. He would help her most — and himself — by staying focused on the task at hand.

Within moments (although it felt like hours), Joseph was close enough to grip the railing. He hauled himself up and over just as the raft broke the surface.

Exhausted, he drew in a deep, shuddering breath, taking in air for what seemed like the first time in ages as the raft was rollicked by the surrounding rapids. On the other side of the raft, where he had tied their donkey, Joseph noticed the animal give itself a powerful shake, attempting to cast off the water that now covered its hide. Surprisingly, it looked none the worse for wear, having apparently come through the entire episode of submersion with little distress.

A frenzied gasping drew Joseph's attention; Mary — having been towed behind him — was on the outside of the raft and hanging on to the railing for dear life.

Joseph quickly got his arms around her and helped her onboard. A moment later, they flopped down, both drained and frazzled by the last few minutes. Resting against the railing, Joseph put an arm protectively around his wife, who leaned in and rested her head on his shoulder, while at the same time wrapping her arms around him tightly.

THE CARPENTER

Chapter 20

Canius, unsurprisingly, was riled. Not only had the couple slipped through their fingers once again, but he had also lost two more of his men — this time permanently. He didn't know how he knew that, as he hadn't seen their bodies; he just perceived that their earthly lives had come to an end. More surprising than anything else was how quickly it had all happened.

After seeing their quarry attempting to cross the riverbed, the decanus and his men had immediately started running after them. They had quickly begun closing the distance between the two parties, with the fleet-footed Gaius soon taking the lead over his fellow soldiers (despite the hindrance caused by the mud). The rest of their troop had not been far behind when Fabian, the youngest legionary, had stumbled and fallen.

At that juncture, they had been charging forward in a fairly tight-knit group, with Fabian ahead of everyone save Gaius. However, the young soldier's unexpected tilt into the mud caused everyone to the rear to trip over him (or trip over someone who had tripped over him). In brief, everyone but Gaius found themselves down in the muck, which proved difficult to rise from.

That said, Fabian — perhaps to make amends for his clumsiness — was the first to his feet and immediately resumed the chase. He was about midway to what appeared to be a raft (where the couple had seemingly stopped) when the water appeared, with a clamor more deafening than a thousand trumpets.

Canius, who was back on his own feet at that point, quickly ordered a retreat to shore. The soldiers who were still with him rushed to obey. Fabian, on the other hand, seemed frozen by indecision — unsure of which direction offered sanctuary — while Gaius lay spread-eagle in the mud.

That was the last the decanus saw of them as he raced back to shore. Far faster than anyone would have expected, the water struck, causing Canius and his men to withdraw even farther inland than they had intended. Moments later, he sensed that Fabian and Gaius were no more, each gone to a watery grave. And it had all happened in minutes.

Reflecting on how quickly everything had unfolded, something akin to gratitude arose momentarily in Canius. He had initially been livid after falling in the mud; however, because of that tumble, he had actually been closer to shore when the wave hit than he would have been otherwise. In that sense, Fabian's fall had been fortuitous — for everyone but Fabian, that is.

Nevertheless, despite having been fortunate enough to survive the floodwaters, Canius felt the old frustration building. His unit was now down to seven, and the prize had once again eluded them. Moreover, his unceasing exasperation had apparently gone beyond simple mental stress and now manifested itself physically: since leaving the riverbank, his sword hand would occasionally experience tremors (although he kept it hidden from the others).

The only saving grace was that, by some still-unknown means, he could sense the direction that the river was taking the couple. Thus, he and the remainder of his soldiers now marched in continued pursuit of their quarry.

THE CARPENTER

INTERLUDE

The Horde felt cheated.

Once again, the man and woman had been practically within its grasp, but had escaped.

The human agents the Horde currently employed — the soldiers — had come ever so close. With the Horde inside them, insidiously guiding their actions, the legionaries were fully committed to pursuit of the couple, even unto the ends of the Earth. Moreover, the Horde had infused them with certain aspects of its essence, such that the men had been able to unerringly sense (and follow) their designated targets, with minimal need for sustenance. Lastly, it had dulled any aches, illness, or injury the soldiers might feel, so that they would not be hampered or handicapped by pain.

All in all, the legionaries had been well-suited for the task at hand and had come within a hair's breadth of achieving the Horde's goal. However, the ensuing flood had spoiled their opportunity.

Reflecting back on it, the Horde felt that there had been something strange about the deluge. Normally, it would have been able to detect such a large body of water, but it had sensed nothing until the tide came screeching into view — and at that point it was too late. Thus, although the majority of the soldiers escaped the water without incident, two of them drowned.

The loss of human life, however, meant little to the Horde. It was not bound by the same rules of existence, so the deaths of the two legionaries was of little note. After their passing, the portions of the Horde's essence that had possessed the two men simply rejoined its constituent parts residing in the remaining seven soldiers.

In short, the Horde felt little in the way of loss regarding the incident involving the floodwaters. The closest it came to regret was recognition and acknowledgment of the fact that it would only have seven soldiers to carry out its wicked schemes rather than nine.

THE CARPENTER

The only other concession it was willing to make in terms of the flood having an effect was the fact that occupying fewer bodies often meant more conflict from its elemental components. In essence, because the Horde was more than just a single entity, there existed the possibility of a possessed subject receiving contradictory guidance or directives. In those circumstances, the conflict often manifested physically, such as a twitching eye or difficulty speaking.

Or, in the case of the legionary leader, a trembling hand…

THE CARPENTER

Chapter 21

By Joseph's estimation, they made good time. It was not the most leisurely or comfortable of journeys — as evidenced by the fact that they spent most of it soaked to the skin — but the raft traveled at a speed he and Mary could never have matched on foot.

When the raft first broke the surface, the water had been tempestuous and raging, with rain still coming down in torrents. After a short time, however, the downpour stopped, and the turbulence of the river subsided. At that juncture — were it not for the dampness of their clothes and the inability to steer — their sojourn on the river might have been construed as enjoyable.

With nothing to do but huddle together for warmth and talk, the two of them engaged in pleasant and stimulating conversation (or as much as they could under the circumstances) for several hours.

****

Eventually, the raft drifted close enough to land for them to safely disembark. (In fact, their craft seemed to come to rest on a sandbar not far from shore.) Joseph elected to carry Mary, thereby ensuring that her feet did not get any wetter than they already were. Leaving his wife on the riverbank — at the edge of a heavily-forested area — he then went back for the donkey, which was still laden with their possessions.

"Which way?" Mary inquired as her husband trudged back to shore, leading the donkey.

"West," Joseph replied, tilting his chin in the proper direction. "The river brought us well to the south, which is good, but has also deposited us a bit farther east than we had been. All things considered, however, this will noticeably shorten our journey."

Looking in the direction indicated, Mary noticed little more than trees and undergrowth.

"Does that include the time needed to hack a trail?" she asked.

Joseph laughed, a sound his wife found comforting. "It's not that bad. We should be able to…" He trailed off as something caught his attention.

"What is *that*?" he uttered with a frown moments later, pointing at something half-obscured by a nearby bush.

THE CARPENTER

Chapter 22

The object that had caught Joseph's attention turned out to be a two-wheeled cart — essentially, a tumbrel. From all indications, it had been seized by the floodwaters and ultimately washed ashore. However, in Joseph's estimation it had suffered little damage and, with just a few adjustments, could be hitched to their donkey. With that in mind, he took out his tools and turned to the task at hand. (In that regard, they were lucky, for his tools — in fact, all of their possessions — although wet, had come through the recent ordeal essentially intact.)

Before long, Joseph not only had the cart in working order, but yoked to their donkey. He understood that others in his position probably would not have tarried, but in his opinion it was time well spent. The tumbrel wasn't exceptionally large, but had ample room for their items and — more importantly — space for Mary.

As they were about to get underway, Joseph decided to make a quick sweep of the area — just in case the floodwaters had left something else they could use. Most of what he came across had little utility or value: shattered pottery, bent or broken farming implements, and so on. He was just about to give up when he practically tripped over a tightly bound, rolled-up bundle that was about as thick around as his thigh.

It was some type of canvas material, he realized — and then grew excited as he recognized what he was holding: a tent.

Tents were generally made to withstand particular elements, like rain. Thus, because of their waterproof nature, certain items were often bound up inside. As he excitedly unrolled it, Joseph was not disappointed. There was a veritable treasure trove inside: several large blankets that had amazingly remained dry — despite what they must have gone through.

Mary quickly stripped out of her damp clothes (to the extent that modesty allowed, even though Joseph was her husband and kept his back to her). She then draped one of the blankets from the tent over herself. Her spouse mimicked her actions, stepping out of his muggy garments before tossing a blanket loosely over his shoulders. Then, after placing their soggy clothes in the cart, they were finally ready to get going.

With Joseph leading the donkey and his wife riding with her feet dangling off the open rear of the tumbrel, they moved along at a nice pace. The only true difficulty was finding a navigable path that they could follow, as much of the ground was covered with underbrush that they either had to ride roughshod over (bearing in mind Mary's condition) or go around.

Catching a glimpse of the sun between the branches overhead at one point, Mary couldn't help but notice that they seemed to be traveling in a direction other than expected.

"Husband, do we still journey west?" she asked.

"Ultimately," he replied. "At the moment, we travel *north*west."

"Do we detour for a reason?"

"Yes," Joseph confirmed. "At present, although we're creating our own byway, I would prefer to travel along an established road or well-worn path. However, if we head due west — which is roughly the direction of our destination — any road we come across is likely to run north to south. Angling slightly increases the chances that we will cross a thoroughfare running east and west."

Mary nodded, understanding her husband's logic. Once again, he'd displayed a talent for forethought and planning. Impressed, Mary gave him an admiring glance just as Joseph halted, bending down to retrieve something from the ground. It appeared to be a stick, which her husband spent a few moments examining intently before placing it in the cart.

Watching him, Mary felt she knew what he was doing, but didn't ask him to explain his actions. Instead, she decided to address a more pressing concern.

"They're going to follow us, aren't they?" Mary asked, bringing up a subject they had not broached previously — even during their hours of talking on the raft.

"Undoubtedly," Joseph solemnly stated, not needing to ask who Mary was talking about. "They seem to be a single-minded group of men."

"They're not just men," Mary countered. "I saw the eyes of the one who attacked you."

"They were completely black," her husband recalled as he picked up (and then discarded) a fallen tree branch. "I've never seen anything like it."

"That thing that attacked us in the night," Mary said. "That's why his eyes were like that — it's inside them. I could smell it on them."

Reaching for another stick, Joseph's brow furrowed in thought. He, too, had smelled the rank odor that had accompanied the soldier he'd pushed, and now — thanks to his wife — he realized why it had seemed familiar. It was the smell that had lingered after the shadow-fiend had fled following its assault on them.

"Then we'll have to be even more vigilant," Joseph finally declared as he tossed the stick into the cart.

THE CARPENTER

Chapter 23

They didn't speak much more of their pursuers. Joseph seemed focused on tossing twigs, branches, and other pieces of wood into the tumbrel. As the pile of sticks grew, it seemingly confirmed what Mary had suspected: her husband was gathering kindling for a campfire. Bearing in mind the weather conditions (specifically, the earlier rain and flooding), he was obviously being selective and trying to find the driest tinder available.

Wanting to contribute, Mary had Joseph stop the cart and stepped down.

"It's not necessary," Joseph stressed after learning of his wife's intent. "We won't need much more for a fire that will last throughout the night."

"Well, four eyes are better than two," Mary stated. "Besides, I feel a need to stretch my legs."

Joseph shrugged noncommittally in reply. Like himself, Mary undoubtedly had experience in gathering firewood and kindling — it was a chore that almost every child was assigned at some point while growing up. Thus, she surely knew what to look for.

With Mary's help, their assortment of sticks grew even faster, as she was apparently more adept than her spouse at spotting potential kindling. Moreover, her keen eyesight was instrumental in another area: finding food, as demonstrated when she espied what appeared to be a small grove of berry bushes.

The bushes in question were actually about two hundred feet away when Mary spotted them, nestled near several sizable trees across a wide expanse of high grass. Rather than take all of their effects while they investigated and then have to backtrack, Joseph tied the donkey to a nearby shrub. He and Mary then took a small basket from their belongings and, with the blankets still draped across their shoulders, began walking towards the plants the latter had seen, which — much to the couple's delight — did indeed turn out to be berry bushes.

The berries were almost as prodigious a find as the tent, for their provisions had been compromised by the flood. Although some of their fare — for instance, many of the vegetables — still had utility, other items were completely unsalvageable. (An example in this latter category included their bread, which was completely waterlogged and would begin to mold soon.)

Initially, they ate almost as much as they put into the basket. Although neither had complained, the two of them had gone the bulk of the day without eating. As he munched on berries (which were sweet and delicious), Joseph suddenly felt a slight twinge of shame; although two meals per day was the norm — in the morning and evening — Mary was pregnant. That being the case, he probably should have stopped and allowed her to eat something earlier.

On her part, Mary had not been discomfited by the lack of a midday meal. In truth, although she generally maintained a healthy appetite, she never experienced excessive cravings. If there was food available, she ate; if none was at hand, she felt no hunger pangs. It was as if the child inside her knew her dietary circumstances and somehow made adjustments so as not to be a burden. In the present instance, she had not been hungry, but felt her appetite return when she and Joseph reached the berry bushes.

THE CARPENTER

In short order, the basket — which was carried by Joseph — was full, despite the time that they took to fill their bellies as well.

Mary turned to Joseph (who was still eating berries) and gave him a mockingly judgmental stare, saying, "You still gorge yourself, husband. Are you certain you are not with child as well?"

Joseph laughed. "No, but they probably failed to inform you during our betrothal that I am half man, half glutton. You'll need to prepare a feast for me nightly."

"Then I should remove these from your care," she said, taking the basket from his hand, "lest they find their way into your stomach as well."

Joseph started to protest, ready to declare that she shouldn't be carrying the basket in her condition, but his wife cut him off.

"Shhh," she muttered, placing a finger on his lips.

Joseph's eyes went wide in surprise.

"It's not that heavy, and the cart isn't far," she continued, practically reading his mind. "So, in all seriousness, you should eat your fill and then join me when ready."

Smiling, Mary then caressed his face gently and, without waiting for him to reply, turned and began heading back towards the tumbrel. Joseph watched her for a moment, thinking that Mary indeed made a good wife. Then he turned back to the berries, promising himself that he'd only eat a few more before rejoining his spouse.

That said, he'd only popped a few more into his mouth before he began experiencing an odd sensation. It was something akin to what he'd felt the night before when the demonic fiend had attacked, but not quite on the same level. There was the impression of nearby danger, but not the same indication of malice nor the feeling of dread. Slowly looking around, he scanned the area intently.

A gentle breeze moved through the trees. The smell of scented flowers wafted through the air from somewhere nearby. The grass, which was about waist-high, swayed gently back and forth.

And it was then, while looking at the grass, that he saw it.

THE CARPENTER

From Joseph's perspective, it first looked like a brown mound of some sort, although only the top of it was briefly visible as the wind whipped across the greenery. A moment later, it was gone from view, obscured by the height of the grass. However, his momentary glimpse had provided him with the distinct impression of a large, bulky frame.

In addition, although he couldn't see it directly, the way the grass parted — shoved to either side of some body in its midst — made it clear that whatever it was Joseph had spotted was on the move, slowly plodding forward. More importantly, it seemed to be heading directly towards Mary, who was meandering back to the tumbrel.

Immediately anxious, Joseph fervently tried to get his wife's attention.

"Mary!" he hissed, trying not to shout. She was maybe fifty feet from him at that point, but — since she didn't turn — seemingly hadn't heard him.

Moving towards her as quickly as he could without exciting whatever was watching, he tried again. "Mary!"

This time his voice reached her ears. Stopping, she turned and looked back at him with a curious expression.

"Get to the cart!" he rasped, casting a quick look in the direction of the thing in the grass, which was roughly a hundred feet from his wife.

Confused, Mary followed his gaze, and then her eyes widened in alarm. Looking back to Joseph, she nodded vigorously to show she understood before turning and resuming her course, although at a noticeably faster clip.

As his wife marched away, the thing in the grass stopped moving, and Joseph felt himself relaxing as the tension in his body began to vanish. However, his relief was short-lived as the air was suddenly filled with a beastly growling. A moment later, he watched in horror as the grass suddenly began swiftly parting along a course that indicated a direct line to Mary. At the same time, the sound of wild, savage grunting reverberated all around them, accompanied by the rhythmic cadence of hooves thunderously striking the ground, indicating an animal running at top speed.

Joseph immediately realized what was happening: the thing in the grass was charging at his wife. With nary a thought, he broke into a run. Although he had no weapon on his person, he angled himself on an intercept course, intent on protecting Mary and her child at all costs.

Generally, he had always been considered a decent runner and had won his fair share of races while growing up. Now, despite being spurred on by the prospect of harm befalling Mary, he found his pace hindered. Almost instantly, he identified the cause: the blanket.

In an effort to keep his hands free, he had previously tied two ends of the blanket in front of him, allowing the bulk of it to drape off his shoulders like a cape. However, as he now ran, it billowed out behind him, catching the wind almost like a sail and thereby acting as a drag on his celerity.

Joseph considered and promptly discarded the notion of trying to take the blanket off as he ran; doing so would sap both time and energy, neither of which he had to spare. Instead, he redoubled his efforts at running, hoping to increase his speed by sheer will.

It only took moments for everything regarding the blanket to flit through Joseph's mind, and before he knew it, he found himself coming abreast of the animal, which was still hidden by the grass. Thankfully, he found he had judged the angle true in terms of intercepting the beast, but he had no time to congratulate himself. Instead, he launched himself at it.

Joseph turned as he dove through the air, shifting so that his shoulder flew at the thing in the grass. A moment later, he connected with something that knocked the air from his lungs, and at the same time sent him spinning through the air like a leaf in a whirlwind. As he twirled, he heard something like deranged squealing — and then he landed with a bone-jarring thud that momentarily drove all thought from his mind.

For a moment, Joseph just lay there, trying to recall exactly what had happened. He shook his head, slightly disoriented and confused as to how he'd come to be lying on the ground. Then a sound reached his ears — something between a bestial grunt and a squeal — and everything came back.

Animal in grass, he said to himself. *Mary…child…still in danger.*

Spurred by those thoughts, Joseph rose groggily to his feet. Glancing around, he saw that Mary had stopped moving towards the cart. Instead, she stood facing him, her features a mask of concern. He was tempted to give her a smile to show he was okay, but the harsh sound of animal grunting drew his attention.

Turning in the direction of the noise, he was somewhat agitated that he still couldn't lay eyes on what was attacking them. However, he could still track its position by the movement of the grass, and from all indications, the animal was circling around and preparing for another charge.

Joseph was slightly dismayed. He seriously doubted that he had hurt it with his previous antics — running into the thing had been like trying to ram a boulder — but he had hoped a challenge of some sort would run it off. Unfortunately, it appeared that all he had done was anger the beast, as evidenced by the fact that, from the way the grass parted, it suddenly began bearing down on him at full speed.

Joseph scoured the area around him, looking for anything that might serve as a weapon. Ironically, the only thing at hand was the blanket he'd been wearing earlier. (Apparently it had come off after he'd slammed into the animal and gone twisting through the air.) Desperate, he grabbed it and then flung it at the beast, which was almost on him at that point.

It was a futile effort, at best, Joseph realized. A blanket was in no way adequate in terms of arms. Thus, what actually occurred was completely unexpected.

The knotted end of the blanket — the corners Joseph had previously tied together — slunk swiftly towards the ground, slithering well down into the depths of the high grass. Fortuitously, this happened directly in front of the charging animal.

From Joseph's perspective, it appeared as though the blanket suddenly took on a life of its own, first rushing towards him in a way that made him dive wildly aside. As he leaped away, he felt a lancing pain in his leg, but ignored it as he hit the ground and then scrambled swiftly to his feet.

THE CARPENTER

He quickly swept the greenery with his eyes, catching sight of the blanket almost immediately. It dashed haphazardly back and forth, like a living thing completely unsure of the direction it wanted to go. It was almost comical, watching it zigzag in random patterns. Possibly the only thing that kept him from laughing at its antics was the high-pitched squealing that filled the air.

It didn't take much mental effort to discern what was happening. The attacking animal, having raced directly into the blanket, now had its head covered. Unable to see, it was literally running around in blind terror, squealing in fright.

And then, seemingly almost as soon as it began, it was over. The animal in the grass, still charging around at full speed, ran straight into a large, towering tree. The impact was sickening, causing Joseph to wince. The tree itself shuddered, and a mass of leaves suddenly came fluttering down while throngs of birds fled the branches in all directions, chirping and cheeping in panic.

Something touched Joseph's shoulder, causing him to turn with a start. He was relieved to find it was only Mary. Wrapping her arms around him, she suddenly gave him an intense hug, which he returned. A moment later, they separated, and — with fingers intertwined — walked towards the tree the animal had run into.

They approached cautiously, although — based on what he'd seen and heard — Joseph felt there was little to fear. The impact with the tree had not only been forceful, but deadly, in his estimation. As if in support of this, their attacker (or rather, the blanket covering it), had not moved or made a sound since the collision.

Releasing his wife's hand and urging her to stay back, Joseph warily approached the motionless form, which was still covered to a large extent. Displaying more boldness than he actually felt, he reached out a hand and whipped the blanket off, giving them their first real look at the animal that had attacked them.

A massive wild boar.

THE CARPENTER

Chapter 25

They stopped for the day a short time after their encounter with the boar, choosing to camp at a clearing near the top of a hill. They had initially planned to travel a little longer, and had trudged up the hill with the sole intent of using the high vantage point to get a better view of the region. (To be specific, Joseph had hoped it would help them spy a westward route, something that had thus far eluded them.) In that regard, luck was with them; from the hilltop, they did indeed see a road heading west far below them. At that juncture, however, Joseph — declaring the hill to be an adequate campsite — called for a halt.

Decision made, Joseph unhitched the donkey and tied it to a nearby bush with edible leaves while Mary took a jar and backtracked to a small stream they had recently passed. Although they had filled their waterskins at the time (and allowed the donkey to drink its fill), they now required water for other purposes, such as cooking. With that in mind, she hurriedly filled the jar and started back.

Upon her return to camp, she couldn't help noticing that Joseph was visibly relieved to see her. The experience with the boar had unnerved him somewhat, and he'd been fighting the desire to be overprotective, understanding that it could be detrimental to a certain extent. (He'd even insisted on taking the jar to the stream at first, until Mary reminded him that retrieving water was women's work, thereby almost shaming him into letting her go alone.) Instead, he had busied himself in her absence by starting a fire and laying out the clammy clothes they'd previously worn over nearby shrubs and bushes in order to give them adequate space to dry. He'd also attempted to erect the tent, but that was one area where his skills were sorely lacking.

"What is *that*?" Mary asked laughingly, pointing at the tent, which slanted wickedly to one side and appeared on the verge of collapse.

"That would be your bedchamber for the night," her husband replied.

She frowned in mock disapproval. "Clearly you should stick to carpentry."

Joseph burst into laughter, and a moment later, Mary joined him.

"Come," she said after regaining her composure a short time later. "Let me see your leg."

"Eh?" Joseph muttered, slightly confused. A moment later, he remembered and glanced down at his right calf, where a wicked-looking gash was starting to cake over with dried blood.

Following Mary's directions, he sat down on the ground while she poured water on a cloth and began dabbing at the injury. As Mary tended his wound, Joseph reflected back on how it had happened — remembering the pain he'd felt as he dove away from the blanketed boar. Presumably a tusk had momentarily poked out from under the cover, or maybe a jagged hoof had clipped him. Thankfully, the gash wasn't deep nor causing much pain, although it would definitely leave a scar. Regardless, he'd been fortunate to escape with as little injury as he did.

"We were lucky," he found himself saying out loud.

"Hmmm?" Mary muttered, unsure of what he was talking about.

"The boar," he explained. "It was twice my weight. I've seen men torn open by ones only half that size."

"In that case, 'blessed' is probably a better description than 'lucky,'" Mary offered.

Her husband shrugged. "In this instance, I'd argue they mean the same."

Mary didn't disagree with him. As she applied a healing ointment to his leg, she glanced in the direction of the westward path they'd previously spotted, noting that it led to mountainous terrain. She pointed at the region with her chin.

"Will we go over or around?" Mary asked.

"Over," Joseph answered.

"Will it be difficult?"

"No and yes," he replied. Noting a look of confusion on his wife's face, he went on. "There's a pass we can take through the mountains, and reaching it from this side is not particularly difficult. However, the descent once we're through is steep and treacherous. We will have to take great care to avoid injury."

"You've traveled this way before?"

"Again, with my father," he stated with a nod. "There's a mine on the other side of the mountain that we will go by. I've accompanied my father there to buy stone for special tasks. Likewise, I've gone through the mountain pass before, coming to this side to buy prized cedar from a woodcutter."

"I had not considered that carpentry required such extensive travel."

Joseph laughed. "I would not consider a journey of perhaps a week, several times per year, as extensive."

"Of course not," Mary chimed in. "For men, the time spent away is always fleeting, while the time spent at home is interminable."

Joseph threw back his head and laughed heartily.

****

After she finished tending to Joseph's leg, Mary prepared their supper. The meal consisted of the rest of the berries, accompanied by a few vegetables that Mary boiled. Afterwards, they made ready for bed, with Mary entering the poorly-erected tent and Joseph preparing to sleep outside.

Mary had been inside the tent for no more than a few moments, however, before she pulled up the flap and stuck her head back outside.

"It's been poorly raised," she began, "but the tent has ample room for two."

Joseph stared at her for a moment, then said, "I thank you. However, I should be fine out here."

"The night is likely to be chilly, even with the fire," Mary noted. "You're free to join me, husband. I promise I won't bite."

Joseph smiled. "It's a tempting offer, but—"

His words were cut off when Mary, leaning out of the tent, unexpectedly grabbed him by the hand and pulled. He resisted only for a moment, then allowed her to drag him inside.

THE CARPENTER

Chapter 26

They slept next to each other, providing each other with warmth for what did turn out to be a slightly nippy night. Rising early the next morning, they dressed in the clothes Joseph had laid out. Although they were indeed dry, the garments held a bit of chill from the night air.

Joseph worried momentarily that Mary would find the clothes too cold, but she didn't seem to mind. Despite what lay ahead of them, she appeared to be in a cheerful mood. Although they could not know each other yet as man and wife, having her husband beside her while she slept had made her rest easy. As a result, she had awakened in a buoyant mood.

They broke camp quickly and were soon on their way, with Mary again riding in the cart (and this time sitting on the blankets, which she used as a makeshift cushion). Heading downhill for the most part, they traveled at a brisk pace, and it didn't take Joseph long to locate the path heading west.

From that point forward, they encountered few difficulties before reaching the base of the mountains. The road was generally level and unbroken, allowing Mary to enjoy a gentle ride. Also, the weather held, despite a dark and cloudy sky initially giving indications that it might rain. Finally, they met up with other congenial travelers heading in the same direction.

Ultimately, they reached the mountains around mid-morning. Seeing them up close, Mary was struck by how majestic and imposing they appeared. Crossing them seemed a daunting task to her, and she said as much to her spouse.

THE CARPENTER

"We don't have to go all the way over the top of them," Joseph said. "There's a pass, remember?"

Mary nodded, recalling that her husband had said something to that effect. He had also mentioned that the climb up would not be difficult, but looking at the crags and precipices above them, she had trouble giving credence to his assessment.

She need not have worried. The ascent was far less intimidating than it appeared at first blush. Nature had worn down the rocks and features of the mountain in such a way that they formed what almost appeared to be a natural stairway. Consequently, Mary found climbing the mountain to be even easier than Joseph had suggested (although she occasionally had to make way for travelers coming down).

Truth be told, it was her husband who had the more difficult task in ascending the mountainous terrain. Because of the cart, he could not take the path that his wife utilized due to the "steps." Thus, he found himself with the onerous task of getting the donkey and tumbrel up a steeper-than-normal incline. It was probably more than one man could accomplish; fortunately, he had help.

En route to the mountain, Joseph and Mary had become friendly with an elderly man named Micah and his three grown sons: Elihu, Jeriah, and Ofer. Micah was traveling to see his elder brother, who was rumored to be on his deathbed. Not in the best of health himself, Micah's sons had insisted on joining him to ensure that their father reached his destination and returned safely.

Seeing that Micah had trouble with the speed his sons maintained, Joseph had kindly offered to let him ride in the cart with Mary. It was an offer that was gratefully accepted — especially since Joseph also allowed their

107

newfound friends to place as many of their belongings in the tumbrel as could be reasonably accommodated.

Joseph's kindness was repaid when — upon reaching the mountains — Jeriah and Ofer volunteered to help him with the cart while Elihu assisted their father and Mary. (Joseph was only too happy to accept their help, as he had previously pondered whether it would be necessary to abandon the tumbrel rather than try to get it to the pass.) Thus, with everything strapped down as well as possible, the three men tackled the arduous burden of getting the cart up the mountainside.

Mary kept an eye on her husband and his helpers while going up the steps with Elihu and Micah. Truth be told, she didn't need much assistance herself (which was fortuitous, considering that Elihu practically had to carry his father).

"They'll be fine," Elihu assured her, after noticing Mary's constant glances at her husband as they climbed. "This side is nothing. The descent, once we get through, is where the danger lies."

Mary looked at him, curiosity plainly evident on her face. "You've been this way before?"

Elihu nodded. "Many times. I used to work in the mine on the other side."

"But no longer?"

"No," he confirmed, shaking his head. "Simply scaling the slopes every day is hazardous enough, but working in the mine comes with its own set of perils. Sometimes you'll bore into a pocket of poisonous vapor that kills the moment you inhale it. Or the tunnels will collapse and bury you alive in moments, although that is sometimes the result of tremors and earthquakes. And even if they don't collapse completely, they can cause the earth to shift, creating threats on the surface like rockslides. Ergo, even if you make it safely out of the mine after a day's labor, you're still not completely out of jeopardy."

"It strikes me as odd that one would undertake such a dangerous profession," Mary observed.

"It pays well," Elihu stated, "although most of the work is actually done by slaves."

"Still, no amount of money is worth your life."

Elihu nodded. "Agreed, which is why I quit and went back to farming — and not a moment too soon. Three days after I left, there was a cave-in right in the area where I'd been working. Everyone perished."

Stunned by what she'd heard (and how close Elihu had come to death), Mary's mouth almost fell open. Nevertheless, she kept moving, although the conversation at that juncture moved to less disturbing topics.

THE CARPENTER

Chapter 27

They reached the pass without incident (for which Joseph was thankful, as there were several times when keeping the cart moving forward seemed more trouble than it was worth). Mary, Elihu, and Micah had actually arrived first, and then waited patiently for the other three to join them. Afterwards, they journeyed through the pass as they had to the mountain, with Mary and Micah riding, while the four younger men walked.

Although it followed a winding path, the pass had enough breadth to easily accommodate the tumbrel (as well as travelers going in both directions). Moreover, they proceeded at a languid pace, a sure sign that getting the cart up the slopes had been taxing on Joseph, Jeriah, and Ofer. Mary didn't mind, as it made any bumps in the road easier to bear. It also gave her more time to talk to Micah, who was a gifted raconteur. During their ride to the mountain, he had regaled her with anecdotes and tales from his youth; his storytelling continued as they ventured through the pass, making the time fly by. Accordingly, almost before she knew it, Mary realized that they had reached the other side of the mountains, punctuated by her husband dryly announcing, "We're through."

Still seated at the rear of the cart, Mary turned so that she could get a better view of what lay ahead. Looking down from where the pass exited onto the slopes, she noted the mountainside angled downward at a precipitous incline.

"I had thought you might be exaggerating about the descent, husband," she said to Joseph. "Now I see you understated the matter."

THE CARPENTER

"Sadly, my imagination ranks side-by-side with my tent-raising abilities," Joseph said with a wink. "As a result, I lack the ability to embellish descriptions and details, making me a bore to a certain extent."

As his wife snickered at his self-deprecating comment, Joseph glanced down the mountain at what lay ahead of them. Despite addressing the situation with humor, he knew that the descent would be hazardous; one wrong step could send a man tumbling wildly down the slopes. (More to the point, he couldn't shake the image of the cart somehow getting away from him and suddenly barreling down the mountain, careening wildly and then flipping over — with Mary still aboard.) Thus, he spent a moment surveying the terrain for the best possible route, and in the course of doing so he noted something unusual.

Several hundred feet below them and angling diagonally away from their location was a large wooden platform. Joseph knew from previous visits that the platform was built around the entrance to the mine he'd mentioned to Mary the day before. What struck him as odd was the fact that there was now another structure close to the platform. From all appearances, it seemed to be a footbridge that stretched from a spot near the platform to just about the bottom of the mountain.

"Ahhh," said a voice in surprised delight next to Joseph. It was Elihu, who had apparently noticed the walkway as well. In response to Joseph's quizzical expression, he merely smiled and said, "Come on."

****

THE CARPENTER

With the help of Elihu and his brothers, Joseph was able to get the cart — with Mary and Micah still riding — down to the mine. It was slow going, and they had one or two scary moments (such as when the donkey momentarily lost its footing, causing the tumbrel to briefly skid to the side). However, they managed to make it safely to the platform, which was more expansive than Joseph had originally realized.

Once there, he noted that there were a fair number of people present. Some appeared to be workers from the mine, as they carried baskets and such filled with heavy stones. Others appeared to be fellow travelers, either coming up or going down the mountain. (Joseph also observed that several of them took the walkway.)

Among those present, one man in particular stood out: a tall, bulky fellow with a bald head and a beard starting to gray. He seemed to be in charge, barking orders and commands to those around him.

"That would be Itzak — the overseer," Elihu commented, as if reading Joseph's mind. "Let's go speak to him."

Leaving the others with the cart, Joseph and Elihu began making their way through those on the platform.

"I know him from working in the mine," Elihu whispered as they walked. "So — unless you object — I was thinking I should speak for us both."

Joseph nodded in acquiescence. Moments later, they were next to the overseer, standing to the man's right while he engaged in conversation with a traveler.

"A word, if you please, Itzak," said Elihu.

"A moment," the overseer muttered in their direction without deigning to look at them.

"No, not in a moment," Elihu replied. "*Now*, you fat fool."

Suddenly livid, Itzak spun towards Joseph and Elihu, fists balled in anger. He stared at them for a moment, and then burst into laughter, as did Elihu.

"Elihu, you young whelp!" Itzak exclaimed, clapping the younger man on the shoulder. "How are you?"

"I'm well, thanks," Elihu answered. "You're still looking spry."

"Father Time has been kind to me," Itzak declared. "So to what do I owe the pleasure? Have you come to see if there's an opening? We really have all the men we need, but for an old friend I could probably make room, although the pay would be less than what you previously received."

"That's kind of you, but I'm simply passing through," Elihu stated. "However, I couldn't help but notice that you took my suggestion about constructing a ramp up the mountain." He tilted his head towards the footbridge.

"*Your* suggestion?" Itzak stated, looking surprised. "I don't know about *your* suggestion, but the mine owners were enamored with the idea once I told them that it would pay for itself in a year with the money saved on replacing damaged carts, injured workers, and hobbled horses."

"Which is almost word-for-word what I told you when I first mentioned the idea," Elihu retorted. "But I'm not interested in who gets credit for the notion. I'm more interested in its utility. In short, my friend and I" — he gestured towards Joseph — "need to get our families down the mountain and would like to use the walkway."

"By all means, you can use it," Itzak effused.

"Thank you," Elihu said.

"For a price," the overseer added.

Elihu, who had begun to turn away, spun back around to face him. "What?"

Itzak smiled. "After the walkway was completed, travelers were constantly asking to use it. The mine owners suddenly realized that they had an additional source of revenue available."

"So travelers pay a toll to utilize it," Elihu concluded.

Itzak nodded. "Sadly, yes. If it were up to me, I'd charge no one, but the owners are not so benevolent." He leaned forward conspiratorially, whispering, "They are callous men, who care only for wealth."

"I refuse to believe you have no leeway here," Elihu said, shaking his head. "My father's elderly and infirm, while my friend's wife is pregnant. For once, show that you've got a heart in your chest rather than a stone mined from the earth, and let us—"

"Pregnant, did you say?" the overseer blurted out excitedly, interrupting Elihu. "Show me."

Elihu stared at the man in surprise for a moment, then nodded. Although slightly baffled by Itzak's sudden change in demeanor, he and Joseph led the overseer back to where the rest of their party waited.

Once at the cart, Itzak asked Mary to stand. After she complied, the overseer merely stared at her for a few moments, a look of intense concentration on his face.

"I'm sorry," he finally said. "You still have to pay the toll."

"We don't have funds for that," Elihu confessed.

"Then you may have to take your chances," the overseer stated. "But I must warn you: descending the mountainside is treacherous even for the most surefooted of men."

As if in evidence of this, a yelp of terror and anguish suddenly echoed across the slopes. Without warning, most of those present rushed to the edge of the platform and stared down the mountain. Joseph, having managed to end up at the front of the spectators, got a first-hand view of what had drawn everyone's attention: a man (who had been either coming up or going down the slopes) had apparently slipped, and — as everyone watched — went tumbling swiftly and violently down the mountainside.

Joseph stared in horrid fascination as the man, crying out in both fear and pain, flipped and rolled rapidly downhill, occasionally even seeming to bounce off the ground. It put Joseph in mind of a circus performer who had mastered the art of performing in-air acrobatics but never learned how to land. Giving credence to this perception, the man performed a somersault in mid-air — then came down squarely on his head. At that point, his clamoring came to an abrupt halt — which was probably a mercy since a few moments later he landed awkwardly on his left arm, after which it seemed to stick out at an unnatural angle.

Thankfully, the gruesome spectacle came to an end shortly thereafter, with the man ceasing to tumble and instead skidding to a halt on his back. To no one's great surprise, he didn't move or make a sound.

Clearing his throat, Itzak turned back to Joseph and Elihu. "As I was saying, you can pay the toll or take your chances on the slopes, but the mountain is unforgiving."

No one said anything. Itzak shrugged and began to turn, apparently ready to resume his normal routine.

"How about an exchange instead?" Elihu offered.

Chapter 28

The bargaining was swiftly completed. Rather than hand over coin for the right to use the footbridge, Elihu negotiated a deal whereby they would pay in service. In essence, they would use the tumbrel to haul a load of stone — allegedly marble — from the mine down the mountain. This would allow Itzak to save time and effort (as well as money) by not having to send his own people to perform the task.

"We'll be taking the stones from the mine about halfway down," Elihu said, after pulling Joseph aside to discuss the details of the bargain he'd struck.

"Why only halfway?" asked Joseph.

"Because Itzak's afraid that if we reach the bottom with his property, we'll try to run off with it."

Joseph was incredulous. "He actually said that?"

Elihu chortled. "No, but he didn't have to. I know how he thinks. What he actually said was that's the juncture at which they usually load their own carts." Elihu pointed at a spot well down the walkway — several hundred feet, at the very least — as he spoke. "The horses they use don't do well at higher elevations, so that's about as far up as they come."

Joseph stared at the area indicated. "The footbridge is well above the ground at that point."

"Yes," Elihu agreed with a nod. "The walkway slopes downward just like the mountainside, but much more gradually. As a result, the difference in height between the walkway and the ground increases as you go down."

Joseph nodded in understanding, comprehending in full what Elihu was explaining. Then he frowned as he contemplated the logistics of what they'd be attempting.

"Exactly how is this supposed to work?" he asked. "Do the two of us and your brothers take the cart down, while Mary and your father take the walkway?"

Elihu shook his head emphatically. "No, you need to stay with your wife. It's part of the deal."

Joseph gave him a confused look. "I don't understand."

"Itzak insisted on it. The two of you will remain here while my brothers, father, and I take the cart down."

"Another strategy to avoid theft, I suppose?"

Elihu shrugged. "Again, he never said that, but it's probably a safe assumption." Unexpectedly, Elihu's brow furrowed. "However, I advise you to be wary."

His tone was incredibly somber — almost ominous.

"Why?" Joseph asked, alarmed. "What do you know?"

Elihu simply stared at him for a moment, then let out a deep breath. "Nothing for sure. It's just that Itzak…" He trailed off, glancing at the overseer.

Following his companion's gaze, Joseph saw that Itzak had moved back to where they'd originally seen him and was speaking to what appeared to be an underling. The subordinate gave a curt nod, and then dashed towards the entrance to the mine.

"He may seem somewhat congenial," Elihu went on, "but he's an unsympathetic individual with a greedy and covetous nature, and a love of money that is legendary. The way he stared at your wife — I know that look. He's plotting something, so stay close to Mary."

"I plan to," Joseph assured him. "Just meet us at the bottom of the walkway with the cart."

"The bottom?" Elihu repeated, a sly look on his face. "I was thinking more along the lines of the halfway point."

THE CARPENTER

Chapter 29

Joseph and Mary stood on the platform as Elihu and his brothers took the donkey and cart down the mountain. Micah once again rode in the tumbrel, although he now shared the space with a hefty supply of ore taken from the mine, as well as the two parties' respective possessions.

Elihu, who was most familiar with the terrain and the task at hand, took the lead in guiding the donkey down the slopes. Having performed similar work while employed at the mine, he seemingly had an aptitude for selecting the safest course — something Joseph had noticed when they had initially trekked from the mountain pass to the platform. Now, the former miner kept his group moving down at an appropriate angle and a suitable speed, with his brothers on either side of the cart in case anything went awry.

As Elihu's party had a larger area to traverse, it understandably took longer for them to reach their designated stopping point than it had to reach the platform earlier. However, despite a few scares (at least one of which made Mary gasp), they arrived essentially unscathed at their destination.

"They made it," said a voice to Joseph's left, sounding a bit surprised. It was Itzak. Apparently Joseph had been so engrossed in watching the progress of his companions that he hadn't even noticed when the overseer approached and took a position next to him. Joseph spared him a quick glance, then turned his attention back to his comrades.

There was a horse and cart already there (apparently waiting for Elihu's group), along with roughly a half-dozen men who presumably worked for Itzak. As Joseph watched, Micah's sons began shuffling back and forth between the two carts. At that distance, he couldn't quite make out what they were doing, but he suspected they were moving the stones to the waiting cart. (Apparently Itzak was determined to get his money's worth.) At the same time, one of the men near them raised a long pole with a red flag tied on the end and waved it. Itzak then turned and nodded to a subordinate, who reciprocated by waving a similar flag.

Seeing all this, Joseph assumed that their use of the footbridge was now sanctioned. Without waiting for permission, he began maneuvering Mary quickly towards a nearby gangplank that connected the platform to the walkway.

Although broad enough for the two of them to walk side-by-side, the plank wobbled slightly as they stepped onto it, given the impression of shoddy assembly. In fact, to Joseph's trained eye, the entire walkway — from the supporting framework to the decking to the rails — seemed put together in haphazard fashion. That said, although the workmanship was deplorable at best, he was confident that they could traverse the walkway in safety.

The gangplank angled up to the footbridge, and they had just reached the top of it and stepped onto the walkway proper when Joseph and Mary found their way barred by a man, standing a few feet away from them, who was even taller and more rotund than Itzak. Joseph had noticed him earlier and had assumed, rightly, that the man was a guard, posted on the footbridge to keep those who hadn't paid from taking the walkway. Somewhat confused, Joseph looked back towards Itzak, only to find the overseer staring at him with a smug look on his face.

"Someone wants a word with you," Itzak called out.

That's when Joseph noticed who was standing next to the overseer: three Roman legionaries — one of whom he immediately recognized. It was the decanus who'd threatened to slit his throat in Uri's barn.

THE CARPENTER

Chapter 30

Canius got great satisfaction out of seeing the look of shock on Joseph's face. Obviously the man was not expecting to see him here. Had their positions been reversed, the decanus would have felt the same.

In essence, Canius and his men had covered an expansive amount of ground in roughly a day. This had been accomplished by traveling nonstop since the encounter at the riverbed, at the expense of food, rest, and even sleep. The soldiers couldn't match the speed of the raft that had carried Mary and Joseph away, but they had made up for the shortcoming by running almost the entire time — an impressive feat considering that they had done so in full armor and loaded with all their gear.

Knowing their quarry's ultimate destination, the soldiers had also angled west, hoping to stay ahead of the couple. In addition, they still had the benefit of being able to track Mary and Joseph by some extra-sensory means, although the ability seemed to be diminishing in that they only had an idea of the region — not the specific location — of their targets. All in all, the combination of their knowledge and efforts had led them to the west side of the mountain range, where a mine was located.

Once there, Canius had wasted little time trudging up the walkway and making their mission known to the mine overseer, a portly buffoon called Itzak. The man seemed cooperative and even inquired about a reward for relevant information. It implied that his assistance could be assured for a price, but the truth of the matter was that Itzak was a Jew — like those they sought — and therefore wasn't to be trusted.

123

THE CARPENTER

Thus, after not even deigning to answer the question about a reward, the decanus had made what he viewed as a prudent decision and ordered four of his men to wait at the base of the mountain while two others remained with him. He had then told Itzak that he wanted to inspect the mine — ostensibly to make sure that their quarry hadn't taken refuge (or been offered shelter) inside.

The overseer had complied, designating one of his subordinates as a guide and commanding him to allow Canius to inspect at his leisure. Ergo, the decanus and the two legionaries at his side had entered the mine.

Under other circumstances, Canius probably would have ordered the two soldiers with him up to the mountain pass and then entered the mine without escort. However, Jewish hatred of Rome was well-known, and even a veteran soldier could fall victim to an "accident" in a dark, underground chamber. On the other hand, such misfortune was unlikely to occur with three soldiers present. Although this meant there was no one watching the pass, the presence of the remaining legionaries at the bottom of the mountain gave him little cause to worry that the couple they sought would slip by.

In truth, it hadn't taken them long to get a quick look at the interior of the mine. Although they didn't investigate every corridor or alcove, Canius quickly perceived (by some method he couldn't explain) that the couple they pursued was not present. He had then insisted on being led to the exit.

Unfortunately, their guide at that point seemingly became lost. This resulted in the three legionaries spending more time underground than they had intended. Angry at this turn of events and with his frustration mounting, Canius was on the verge of drawing his sword and running their guide through when another of Itzak's workers appeared with news that the man and woman the soldiers were after had appeared. The new arrival then led the legionaries back to the entrance of the mine.

As he stepped into the light, the decanus found himself greeted by Itzak, who quickly guided him to one side, pointing towards the footbridge Canius and his men had traversed up the mountain. On it were the couple he and his men had sought, their way being blocked by one of the overseer's guards.

The man, Joseph, had then turned towards Itzak with a look of bewilderment on his face. The overseer said something to the fellow, but Canius couldn't make out the words. The decanus was so thrilled — so ecstatic — by the thought of finally catching his quarry that his elation essentially drowned out everything else. And then Joseph's gaze slid to Canius himself, and the startled expression on his face was beyond price, in the decanus's opinion.

Immensely pleased at this turn of events, Canius was about to order his men to seize the couple when the ground suddenly shook. It was if the mountain were a living thing — a giant of stone swiftly and unexpectedly rousing from deep slumber.

Having experienced similar events in the past, Canius — struggling to stay on his feet — immediately understood what was happening, and was therefore not the least bit surprised when someone screamed, "Earthquake!"

THE CARPENTER

Chapter 31

Joseph didn't even try to hide his shock at seeing the legionaries. Even moving at their best speed, they shouldn't have been able to travel so far so quickly. And then he remembered: the soldiers weren't just men any more. They were nourished and sustained by some evil force beyond the ken of men.

Although this flitted through his mind in but a moment, he was still so stunned that he might have simply stood there indefinitely, unmoving, had not the ground unexpectedly began convulsing wildly, bringing him back to himself.

Although he staggered slightly himself, Joseph gripped his wife's arm in attempt to steady her as someone bellowed the word, "Earthquake!"

The guard on the bridge, apparently caught in the process of taking a step when the tremors began, lumbered forward, off-balance. Although his own stance was unsteady, Joseph took a position protectively in front of Mary, while at the same time using his body to force her back slightly, letting the guard stagger past. Taking a chance and acting on instinct, Joseph extended a leg and tripped the man. The guard fell forward heavily on to the gangplank, smashing through it entirely. Just a few moments later, the tremors subsided.

Joseph took a moment to look back at the legionaries, who were somewhat stranded on the platform now that the gangplank was no more. The decanus was livid, his face a mask of unbridled fury. The soldier opened his mouth and let out a howl of frustration, a vehement shriek that seemed more fitting to a beast than a man.

At the same time, a deep rumbling began to echo across the mountains, while the ground began to rattle once more, although in a less pronounced fashion than just a few moments earlier. As the rumbling grew in volume, Joseph thought he detected the source of the sound and looked up the mountain, as did a number of people on the platform.

Joseph stared in horror at what he was seeing, as did Mary beside him when she followed his gaze: tons of stones were cascading down the slopes.

The earthquake had caused a rockslide.

Chapter 32

"Run!" Joseph shouted in Mary's ear. With a grip on her arm, he began dashing down the walkway, almost dragging his wife along (or rather, as fast as her condition would allow).

The footbridge swayed slightly as they ran, although whether the result of poor construction, the earthquake, or the rockslide, Joseph didn't know. Thankfully, it was essentially deserted. Joseph couldn't ascertain whether this was the result of people refusing to pay the toll, having fallen off during the quake, or other reasons; he was simply grateful that they basically had an unobstructed path to their destination: the midpoint of the walkway.

"There should be a rope on the footbridge in that area," Elihu had said. "They use it to lower the mined stones — mostly marble — down to the carts below."

Because they hadn't trusted Itzak (which turned out to be a sound display of judgment), they had devised a strategy to avoid taking the walkway all the way to the bottom of the mountain. Instead, the plan was for Joseph to use the rope Elihu had mentioned to lower Mary down and then climb down himself. Their donkey and tumbrel should be waiting below, as that was the juncture at which Elihu and his brothers had transferred the stones they had transported down the slopes.

A bevy of screams and shouts broke in on Joseph's thoughts. Glancing at the slopes as they ran, he saw that numerous people had thrown caution to the wind, racing down the mountain with an army of rocks bearing down on them. They had his sympathy, but he could do nothing for them. In fact, his own plight was essentially the same. (As if he needed a reminder of this, a stone roughly the size of his hand suddenly bounded across his line of sight no more than a foot in front of him.)

Out of a sense of caution, Joseph glanced behind them as they ran. What he saw should not have surprised him: a vambrace-covered arm swinging up onto the footbridge. The legionaries were climbing up to the walkway. Joseph turned back to the path ahead of them, trying to put the notion of how close the soldiers were out of his mind.

Moments later, he saw the rope, one end of which was tied to a metal ring bolted to the decking. Hurrying to the spot where it was located, he scooped it up, then took a moment to peer over the side of the walkway. As planned, the donkey and cart were below them, maybe twenty feet down, but their companions were nowhere in sight. More importantly, the donkey — although tethered to the understructure of the walkway — was plainly in distress and trying its best to break away, most likely because of the rockslide.

Deciding that the disappearance of Elihu's family could remain a mystery for the moment, Joseph swiftly tied the rope under Mary's arms. After making certain it would hold, he helped her over the railing and began lowering her to the ground. Her head had just dropped below the level of the walkway's decking when Joseph heard and felt a furious pounding emanating from the direction they had come. Looking towards the source of the sound, he saw a legionary — presumably the one he'd seen climbing up to the walkway — bearing down on him with his sword raised overhead, apparently intent on striking a killing blow.

129

THE CARPENTER

Aware that he held the life of Mary and her unborn child in his hands, Joseph didn't move. Intent on protecting his wife and the baby she carried, he continued lowering Mary to the ground as swiftly as he could, even as the charging soldier drew near.

The soldier was close enough for Joseph to see his eyes — all black, like back at the river — and the latter was steeling himself for the blow he knew was coming when something smashed into the legionary's head.

No, not smashed into, Joseph discerned a moment later. *Took off…*

He hadn't immediately realized what had just happened, but the truth had quickly dawned on Joseph: a rock about the width of his thigh had seemingly bounded down the mountain (along with innumerable others) and careened into the soldier's skull, severing his head from his body almost as neatly as with a blade. The body stood there for a moment, then toppled over backwards and began gushing blood across the decking. Joseph ignored it and continued lowering his wife to the ground.

Moments later, he felt the rope go slack. Peering over the edge of the walkway, he saw Mary in the back of the cart. She waved to him, then quickly shimmied out of the rope tied around her, pulling it up over her head. As she did so, the donkey bucked wildly, causing her to plant her hands on the sides of the tumbrel to brace herself.

Grasping the rope tightly, Joseph began to climb over the railing, intent on descending to the ground as quickly as possible. At that moment, two things happened almost simultaneously.

First, with its hide being pelted by stones from the rockslide, the donkey lurched wildly, breaking away from the spot where it was tethered. It then began to gallop down the mountain, with the cart (and Mary) in tow.

At the same time, Joseph spotted another soldier coming at him from the same direction as the one who had been killed. More to the point, it was the decanus, and there was a murderous bent to his expression and stride.

Joseph scrambled back onto the footbridge and began sprinting towards the bottom of the mountain. He didn't look behind him; there was no need. It was death behind him — no more, no less. Instead, he focused his attention on the tumbrel, glancing over the side of the footbridge every few seconds.

As luck would have it, the donkey ran a course parallel to the walkway — right next to it, in fact. However, its speed, unsurprisingly, was in excess of his own, and the cart was visibly pulling away from him.

Much like the donkey had earlier, Joseph found himself being peppered by rocks and stones from the rockslide as he bolted down the footbridge. He held an arm up in an effort to shield himself from the worst of the assault, at the same time squinting not just to protect his eyes from pebbles and pellets, but also from an expanding cloud of dust being raised by the cascading rocks.

Out of the blue, a boulder the size of a calf slammed into the footbridge about ten yards ahead of him, rocking the entire structure and ripping a chasm roughly twelve feet wide in the decking. Although thrown off-balance, Joseph managed to stay on his feet. Most crucial, however, was the fact that he kept running, planting a foot and managing to clear the breach in a single leap. Landing on the other side, he kept running almost without breaking stride, almost giddy over the jump he'd just made.

Unfortunately, his joy was short-lived, as a few moments after his own leap, he heard a distinct metallic clattering. He didn't have to turn around to know what it meant: the legionary behind him had successfully jumped the gap as well.

Starting to feel winded and desperate, Joseph looked down towards the cart and saw that it was even farther away than he'd suspected. He was never going to catch it. Even worse, ahead of him he saw something that filled him with dread: another legionary. They had him surrounded. Breathing heavily, Joseph prayed for strength.

Suddenly the footbridge shook, as if pummeled by another boulder. At the same time, an unexpected neighing drew Joseph's attention. Looking down, he noticed that the donkey had stopped running and had reared up on its hind legs, as if startled.

Sensing an opportunity, Joseph scanned the area for anything that might be helpful. Directly ahead and stretching towards him was another length of rope, much like what had been located at the midpoint of the walkway. Directly below him, he saw the donkey; the animal had recovered from its start and begun moving again. That being the case, he only had seconds to put the plan that had just occurred to him into motion — especially with the two soldiers closing in from the front and behind.

Looking at the rope as he ran, he judged the length that he needed, and then — bending low as he dashed towards it — he grabbed it at the point he had mentally tagged. Gripping the cord in white-knuckled desperation and almost without breaking stride, he then made a flying leap over the railing just as the two soldiers reached him.

Chapter 33

It was only after he was airborne, with the cart directly below him, that Joseph suddenly identified an essential — potentially *fatal* — flaw in his plan: he had never checked to see if the other end of the rope was tied off.

Thankfully, he didn't have time to fret in regard to the oversight, as within moments his movement changed from a straight descent to the ground to an arc. Feeling relief as he curved through the air, he made fervent hand motions to his wife — urging her to move to the side as his momentum brought him over the cart — then dropped down a bit awkwardly next to her.

As Mary gave him a fierce hug, Joseph glanced up at the walkway. The two soldiers were staring at them menacingly. A moment later, he lost sight of them as dust from the rockslide engulfed that portion of the footbridge.

****

Although it was a bit of a rollicking ride, they managed to make it safely to the bottom of the mountain. In Joseph's opinion, this was due in large part to the lower portion of the mountain not being quite as steep as what they had encountered at higher elevations. (It also didn't hurt that the donkey seemed to intuitively know which way it should go.)

That said, although they had seemingly outrun the rockslide (although not by any great length, in Joseph's opinion), they hadn't escaped its effects altogether. Namely, the dust cloud it spawned rolled downhill and

134

caught up to them, requiring that they wrap their faces protectively and making it difficult to see. That being the case, Joseph had thought it futile to try to guide the donkey. Joking to Mary that the animal had brought them safely down the mountainside, he decided to give the donkey its head and allow it to choose their path.

With nothing to do for the nonce, Joseph felt himself relaxing and unexpectedly realized that he had been incredibly tense. He closed his eyes, thankful for a small respite from what felt like days of perpetual conflict. Within moments, he was asleep.

Chapter 34

A day that had started out with great promise had not ended well for Itzak the overseer.

Things had begun well enough, with workers in the mine locating a new vein of valuable ore. Although the owners of the mine were the ones who would profit most from the find, Itzak would make certain that he prospered from it as well.

Next, a wealthy merchant caravan had come through early in the day. Wary of risking their goods on the mountain's hazardous slopes, they had allowed Itzak to gouge them mercilessly, paying well above the going rate for passage via the walkway.

In addition, some young fool with more coins than sense had paid in advance for his younger brother (who was traveling a day behind him) to use the walkway when he arrived. Itzak had laughed, thinking how funny it would be when he charged the younger sibling the full toll anyway.

Yes, the day had started out well indeed. Until the soldiers arrived.

First of all, they used the walkway — without paying — to get up the mountain. The fact that anyone felt they could use the footbridge without charge rankled the overseer. That said, he was not so foolish as to think he could challenge a contingent of legionaries. Thus, he had bit his tongue and merely listened while the leader of the soldiers, Decanus Canius, explained that they were searching for a man and his pregnant wife.

Itzak, with a nose for understanding when information was valuable, had then asked about a reward. The decanus added insult to injury at that juncture by not even deigning to give him a response. In fact, the question seemingly made Canius suspicious, as he then asked to inspect the mine.

Irritated by the Roman's behavior but understanding that his options were limited, the overseer had provided a guide to take the decanus and several of his men into the mine while the remainder took positions at the foot of the mountain. However, with his anger smoldering, Itzak had surreptitiously given the guide instructions to make sure the soldiers got "lost" in the mine. (Maybe that would make them treat him with a little respect.)

In the meantime, it seemed like the overseer's pendulum of luck began to swing back to the positive, as the quarry sought by the soldiers seem to fall right into his lap. Unfortunately, Itzak hadn't been able to think of a way to profit from the situation. He didn't know enough about why the couple was being pursued, so he wasn't able to determine how to benefit from the circumstances other than giving the soldiers what they wanted. (And who knew what could happen? Maybe the legionaries would be grateful enough to bestow a reward on him after all.)

With that in mind, Itzak had sent another worker to locate Canius in the mine and tell him that the overseer had found the couple being sought. While he waited, Elihu had approached him with the offer of service in exchange for passage across the footbridge — a bargain to which Itzak acquiesced. (It seemed like an opportunity to gain some advantage from this situation — especially if no reward was in the offing.)

After their companions started the journey down the slopes, the overseer had briefly contemplated simply taking the man and woman into custody. However, he had a limited number of sentries, and he'd already stealthily sent word downhill that Elihu and his people were to be taken (after unloading the cart, of course). If he utilized too many of his people for such work, there'd be no one left to attend to conventional tasks, such as guarding the walkway.

All things considered, Itzak felt that simply having the couple within reach should be enough to earn the favor of the Romans. Such was his thinking when, a short time later, the decanus exited the mine entrance and stepped back onto the platform. At that juncture, the overseer proudly pointed to the walkway, where the targeted couple now found their way blocked by one of the overseer's more imposing guards. From the look on Canius's face — especially after Itzak called out to the couple — the notion of a reward suddenly didn't appear that far-fetched. And then disaster struck.

First, there was the earthquake. Almost immediately thereafter came the rockslide. Taking shelter just inside the mine entrance, Itzak had barely escaped with his life (although some of his subordinates were not so fortunate).

Afterwards, when he had left the mine, he surveyed the damage to everything — the platform, walkway and more — and found it to be extensive. He was still assessing the cost to replace everything when he noticed someone approaching him, walking across the remains of the platform. It was Decanus Canius, covered in dust but with his sword drawn and an intense look on his face.

Itzak immediately recognized that he was out of his depth. All signs pointed not just to Canius being livid, but looking to take his anger out on someone.

"H-honorable Decanus," Itzak began, "a thousand apologies—"

He got no further before Canius, incensed and fuming, swung his blade, neatly lopping the overseer's head off his shoulders.

No, the day did not end well for Itzak at all…

THE CARPENTER

INTERLUDE

The Horde took some degree of pleasure in the death of the overseer, who had clearly delayed in informing the Horde's human agents of the presence of their quarry. The Horde had initially sensed in the man a towering streak of greed and shrewd cunning, but had thought it could be used to its advantage. Instead, the overseer's self-serving nature had been costly — both to the Horde and, ultimately, the overseer himself.

That said, the man's death offered little solace to the Horde. Once again, it had been ever-so-close to its prey, only to have the prize slip from its grasp.

In retrospect, the Horde found itself once again somewhat bewildered by the turn of events. As with the flood the day before, it should have inherently sensed the earthquake before it occurred, as well as the ensuing rockslide. Instead, it had been aware of neither before the events actually unfolded.

The disruption of its inherent abilities was maddening to the Horde. It had never before found itself — its plans — so foiled and frustrated, and certainly not on so consistent a basis.

Once again, the Horde blamed the unborn child for its growing deficiencies and shortcomings. Ever since the babe had entered its sphere of knowledge and influence — from the moment the Horde had detected that first seraphim — its natural powers and prowess had seemingly started to wane, beginning with its impotence in tracking the pregnant woman. Thus, the Horde was convinced that, if it could only kill the child, everything would return to normal.

Unfortunately, getting rid of the unborn baby was becoming more challenging with each passing moment, starting with the fact that the Horde was now having difficulty tracking its prey. The unerring accuracy with which it had been able to pinpoint the location of the couple just a day earlier was fading, such that now it only had a general idea of their location. (Upon reflection, it was as if the encounter at the riverbed had resulted in some force or power becoming aware of the Horde's ability to stalk its prey and was actively thwarting it.) At the rate it was diminishing, the Horde would only be able to trail the couple for another day or two, at most.

Next, the Horde now found itself down to four human agents. Although it had begun the excursion on the mountain with seven legionaries, one had been killed when the earthquake caused a fissure to open beneath his feet and swallow him. Another had been jostled by the tremors and fallen from the mine platform; despite wearing armor, bouncing and rolling down the steep mountainside had left him battered and broken, with little life left in him. A third had been decapitated by a stone during the rockslide — frustratingly, while within arm's reach of the husband being pursued.

As before, the Horde aspects fleeing the dead and dying bodies joined the rest of its constituent elements in the remaining soldiers. Again, this would make control of its agents more difficult, and for a moment the Horde considered taking possession of others in order to replenish its numbers as well as minimize the innate conflict from having so few controlled by so many. Ultimately, it rejected the notion, deciding that its energy was better spent focusing on tracking the child as opposed to trying to control more bodies.

After all, tracking — and killing — the child was all that truly mattered now.

THE CARPENTER

Chapter 35

Joseph awoke to the sound of running water and voices. Opening his eyes, he found himself staring up into the branches of a large tree. The limbs swayed slightly as the result of a gentle breeze, thereby allowing sunlight to peek through sporadically. Still in the back of the cart, he sat up and stretched while looking around.

He was in a forested area, shaded by a number of sizable trees. Nearby was a brook — the source of the water he'd heard. Their donkey, detached from the cart, was drinking its fill. Not far from it stood Mary, chatting amiably with Elihu and another young man.

Joseph exited the cart, the movement drawing the attention of Mary and the two men.

"You're awake!" his wife said excitedly. Smiling, she quickly began walking toward him, followed by Elihu and his companion.

Once close enough, Mary gave him a hug, which Joseph happily returned before turning to the two men.

"It's great to see you," Elihu said with a grin, clapping Joseph on the shoulder.

"Likewise," Joseph stated sincerely. "I wasn't sure what happened to you."

"Itzak happened," Elihu replied. "As I mentioned, he was up to something. When we got the stones down the slopes, there were guards waiting for us. We were told to move the stones over to the waiting cart and then they ordered us to go with them."

"That was on Itzak's command," said the young man with Elihu.

Upon closer inspection, Joseph realized that the fellow was little more than a boy. He gave Elihu an inquisitive look.

"This is Hiram," Elihu explained. "He works at the mine."

"Work*ed*," Hiram clarified, causing Elihu to laugh.

"I stand corrected," Elihu said. "After today, he's terminating his service."

"Elihu is allowing me to travel with his family," Hiram said, "and when they return home, he says I can work on their farm."

"However, he may find me a sterner taskmaster than Itzak," Elihu joked. "But speaking of the overseer, Hiram has some information you may find interesting."

****

Joseph listened intently as Hiram told of how a group of Roman soldiers had arrived at the mine shortly before Elihu and Joseph had shown up with their respective families. The legionaries had been looking for a man and his pregnant wife, and were certain they were in the region. So, while a few of them took positions at the base of the mountain, several others went to inspect the mine. Thus, it was only through fortuitous timing that Joseph and Mary had missed being intercepted by the soldiers. Once aware of the couple's presence, however, Itzak had seemingly begun scheming.

"In the end, he decided to hand you over to the soldiers," Hiram said.

"Knowing Itzak, he was probably hoping for a reward," Elihu added.

"But if he just wanted me and Mary, why bother seizing you and your family?" Joseph asked him.

It was Hiram who answered, saying, "He didn't know what they'd do when the soldiers took you, so he tried to get them out of the way."

"How do you know all this?" Joseph asked.

Hiram cast his eyes down shamefully, muttering, "I'm the one who passed his orders on to the guards."

"Truth be told, my immediate thought was to resist," Elihu admitted. "But I couldn't risk my father being hurt, so we complied and let them lead us away. But we hadn't gone far before the earthquake happened, and at that point everyone began running for their lives — especially in light of the rockslide that followed."

Joseph nodded in understanding. "So, are all of you okay?"

"We're fine," Elihu assured him. "We had to run like the devil himself was behind us, which wasn't easy, burdened with all of our possessions, and poor Father slung across Ofer's shoulders like a bale of hay."

They all laughed at the imagery, although Joseph knew from experience that it had to be terrifying at the time.

"That reminds me," Elihu said. "Your belongings are right there."

He pointed to the side of the cart where, as stated, all of Mary and Joseph's effects sat on the ground. Somehow, they had escaped Joseph's notice when he'd exited the tumbrel.

"Thank you," Joseph stated emphatically. In truth, bearing in mind all that had recently happened, he hadn't even thought about their possessions (although he would have missed them sorely later). "I can't believe you were even mindful of this with everything that was happening."

Elihu shrugged. "When the soldiers ordered us to come with them, we simply took everything from the cart and they didn't try to stop us. Following the earthquake and rockslide, a wise man would have discarded any excess weight, but the sons of Micah are known far and wide for their lack of common sense."

This caused another round of laughter.

After regaining his composure, Elihu said, "Truth be told, I believe we were all too terrified to even think straight, so the notion of dropping anything never occurred to any of us. Personally, the only thing that occurred to me was to run, and we were fortunate that we were already well down the mountainside, and the Almighty gave strength to our limbs."

"Well, words can't express how grateful I am for your efforts," Joseph admitted earnestly.

"Oh," Mary chimed in, "don't forget to tell him how you found us."

Elihu laughed again. "It was shortly after the dust cloud reached the bottom of the mountain. Basically, your donkey and cart almost trampled me."

Joseph was aghast. "I'm sorry. I never—"

"It's okay," Elihu interjected. "It was dusty and I know you didn't see me. Truth be told, I was only half-certain it was you — and from what I could tell no one was driving the cart — but I decided to follow just to make certain. Along the way, I came across Hiram, whom I knew from my time as a miner, although he was just a boy then — not the man you see today."

Hiram's cheeks began to turn red, making Elihu chuckle.

"Anyway," Elihu continued. "I went in the direction I'd last seen you headed and eventually came across your wheel tracks. Needless to say, I'm glad the two of you managed to get safely away."

"As are we," Joseph added. "Your scheme didn't go exactly as planned, but worked out well enough — although we were fortunate not to flip over at the rate the donkey was galloping downhill."

"That's probably a function of the path it was on," Hiram explained. "Even before the walkway was constructed, there was a route of sorts that was used by horses and carts to come up and down the mountain. In fact, that's part of the reason why the footbridge was built where it was — to give easy access to carts on that path. The walkway actually runs right next to it. But, although it's still at a steep angle, all the traffic over the years has made that particular path worn and smooth to a certain extent, unlike other parts of the mountainside."

"Then I suppose we're blessed in that the donkey didn't stray from that path," Mary noted.

"It was probably just following the scent of other horses that use that same route," Elihu suggested. "Quite possibly the one hitched to the cart we loaded just before being taken away, although that animal bolted away from its handler as soon as the tremors started."

"I'd be shocked if there was a living creature that wasn't bolting at that point," Mary opined facetiously, causing everyone to snicker again.

THE CARPENTER

Chapter 36

Mary and Joseph spent a little more time talking to Hiram and Elihu before the two men departed. Elihu's family was aware that he'd gone to find the couple and that he would catch up with them on the road. However, their destination lay in a different direction than that of Joseph and Mary. Thus, they had parted ways, hoping that their paths would cross again one day.

After the two men were gone, Joseph and Mary quickly readied themselves to leave also. By Joseph's estimation, it had been several hours since the incident at the mountain. However, now aware that the legionaries could move quickly, he was anxious to get underway.

Assuming the donkey had grazed enough to fill its belly and drank enough to slate its thirst, he quickly hitched it back to the cart. After that, it was simply a matter of piling their belongings into it, and at that point they were ready to get going (although they did take a moment to shake the excess dust from their clothes).

****

They traveled the rest of the day without incident. Although Joseph urged Mary to ride in the tumbrel, she preferred to walk — quite often next to her husband, holding his hand.

Back at the walkway, when the donkey had suddenly taken off with her in the cart, she had found herself incredibly alarmed at the thought of losing Joseph. In just a few days, he had become an indispensable part of her life, and — frankly speaking — she could not now imagine a future without him. Thus, she had been incredibly relieved when a hefty rock had vaulted across the animal's path, startling it before smashing into the framework of the footbridge. The donkey had reared up in fright, which had given Joseph enough time to catch up and — much to Mary's awe and amazement — swing down to them.

Looking at him now, she smiled, then sent up a small prayer of thanks that such a man was her husband.

THE CARPENTER

Chapter 37

Unsurprisingly, they stopped just before sundown, choosing a small glade as their campsite. They soon had a fire going, and Mary made them a quick meal of lentils from a nearby plant.

Afterwards, they prepared for sleep, with Joseph eschewing the idea of setting up the tent this time. Despite the nap he'd had earlier, he was tired.

To an extent, he recognized that what he was experiencing wasn't just physical fatigue. This journey was unlike any he'd ever undergone, and it was also taking a toll on him mentally. He needed to rest not just his body but also his mind.

As he closed his eyes, he worried for a brief moment about the legionaries. The celerity they had shown in getting to the mountain in such a short span indicated that the soldiers could move far faster than what nature allowed. It brought to mind the notion that he should perhaps stand guard for a while, but he dismissed the thought almost immediately. Plainly speaking, he would be useless to Mary and the baby if he didn't get some much-needed rest. He'd have to trust the Almighty to keep them safe through the night.

With that thought, he went to sleep, with Mary nestled beside him.

****

It was just after dawn when Joseph awoke to the feeling of cold steel pressed to his throat. He opened his eyes to find a man with a scarred face and scraggly beard

— maybe ten years older than himself — squatting down on his haunches, with a knife to Joseph's throat.

A slight cry drew his attention. Glancing in the direction of the sound, he saw Mary, on her feet and struggling against a burly fellow who held her from behind, gripping her upper arms. Despite his size, the man found the job a little difficult — probably because he only appeared to have a thumb and two fingers on his right hand. A third man, of average height but a little scrawny, deftly twirled a dagger back and forth between his fingers while laughing at the efforts of his stout companion, showing a mouth missing a startling amount of teeth.

Noting his wife's distress, Joseph instinctively began to rise from the ground, only to have his efforts halted by the blade pressing against his throat.

"Easy, friend," said the man with the knife. "Wouldn't want you to have an accident."

"Take whatever you want," Joseph blurted out, recognizing the men as bandits. "Just leave us in peace."

"What a coincidence," chuckled the scar-faced man. "That's exactly what we were thinking." His friends snickered at this.

"About taking what we want, that is," the fellow added. "No promises about leaving you in peace — unless you can give us an extra incentive."

"We don't have any money," Joseph insisted. "We're poor travelers hoping to make our fortune in a new city."

"Truly?" said the man with the blade. "Well, I look around and I see a donkey. A cart. The well-maintained tools of a master craftsman." He scratched his beard as if in thought. "I'll admit it doesn't speak of obscene wealth, but it hints at something more than being a simple beggar."

"The donkey was a gift and the cart we found," Joseph said. "We have food and a few possessions, but little else, I swear."

The man with the blade sighed. "I was hoping it wouldn't come to this, but I guess we need to give you time to reflect on exactly how truthful you've been. So while you think, I think we'll each take turns spending a little time with your wife."

There was a glint in the man's eye and a look on his face that Joseph found appalling. He knew with certainty that these men were wretched, and would no doubt do what they said.

"Wait!" Joseph screeched. "Maybe we do have something."

The man holding the knife smiled. "I thought you might."

"It's over by the donkey," Joseph said, pointing to the beast, which he had tied to a bush after unhitching it the previous evening. "I'll get it."

Joseph started to rise, but again found the blade pressing against his flesh.

"Not you," the scar-faced fellow said. He looked at Mary. "You — wife. Go get it." He then glanced at the burly man who was gripping her arms. "Bijan, go with her."

"It's by the donkey," Joseph called out to Mary as Bijan released her. "Be careful — the animal's rambunctious."

Mary gave him an odd look, her brow furrowing for a moment. Then she quickly nodded and began walking towards the donkey, followed by Bijan.

"For your sake, I hope this isn't a trick," declared the man with the blade.

Joseph didn't respond. He just lay there, waiting and hoping that his wife had understood the hint he'd given. Although he couldn't see her from his angle on the ground, a few moments later he heard Mary say, "Here."

Almost immediately thereafter, he heard the donkey bray insanely. At the same time, an odd noise rang out — almost reminiscent of a thick tree branch swiftly and violently splintering. This was followed by the sound of something large and heavy hitting the ground.

Looking in the direction Mary had gone, the scar-faced man muttered, "What the…"

Sensing his chance, Joseph jerked his hand up and gripped the wrist of the hand holding the blade to his throat. Whipping the bandit's hand up and over his head, he then yanked on it hard. The scar-faced man, who had still been on his haunches, was sent sprawling.

Joseph began scrambling to his feet, but had only just gotten his knees under him when he found the third bandit — the scrawny one — rushing at him, dagger raised. Almost without thinking, Joseph leaped at the man feet-first. He managed to plant his feet on his opponent's chest and kicked off.

Joseph fell to the ground as his kick sent the lanky bandit staggering back. Then, seeming to trip over his own feet, the man fell backwards — right onto the remnants of their campfire which, although low, was still burning.

Almost immediately, the bandit's clothing, dirty and soiled, erupted in flames. Screaming in naked terror, the man struggled to his feet. At that juncture, he was essentially ablaze from head to foot. With smoke spewing from him like a torch, he stood there wailing in absolute anguish for a moment, then started to run.

At that moment, Joseph, who had propped himself up on his elbows, caught movement with his peripheral vision. He hastily rolled to the side just as the bandit with the scarred face dove at him, plunging his knife into the earth exactly where Joseph's heart had been a moment earlier.

The man was incredibly quick. Joseph had barely rolled onto his back again before the fellow was on him, diving on top of Joseph and stabbing down with the knife. Fighting for his life, Joseph caught the wrist of the fellow's knife-hand before the blow could strike.

For a moment, it was a contest of equals, with neither man able to obtain the advantage. Then the bandit shifted his position slightly, putting more of his weight on Joseph. At the same time, he began using both hands to try to force the point of his blade into Joseph's throat.

It was clear that the bandit was experienced in these types of engagements and had positioned himself where it was most advantageous. This became obvious to Joseph as his hands started to tremble with effort. Even worse, the blade started to slowly descend.

The scar-faced man, sensing victory was within his grasp, redoubled his efforts. A moment later, he was smiling with glee as the tip of the knife touched his adversary's throat.

Feeling the cold metal now touching his skin, Joseph prayed to the Heavenly Father for strength. Suddenly, the bandit jerked slightly and went stiff, with a blank look in his eyes. More importantly, the downward pressure on the blade stopped. And then, to Joseph's surprise, the bandit slowly toppled to the side. As the

153

man fell off him, Joseph saw Mary standing directly behind where the fellow had been, holding the dagger of the bandit who had fallen into the campfire.

The weapon was covered with blood.

"Husband," Mary said. "Are you all right?"

THE CARPENTER

Chapter 38

To the extent it could have been referred to as a plan, Mary had played her role with aplomb. Understanding Joseph's hint, she had gone towards the donkey with a determined stride — as if she knew exactly what she needed to do. Mentally, however, she had been struggling, and literally wringing her hands.

As she did so, she happened to touch a silver bangle on her wrist. It had been a gift from her maternal grandmother, and one of the few truly valuable items that she possessed. And at that moment, her thoughts had coalesced into an actual strategy.

Keeping her hands in front of her, she had furtively slipped the bracelet off. Upon reaching the donkey, she had reached her hands into the thick leaves of the bush where it was tethered as if grabbing something.

Withdrawing her hand, she had then turned and tossed the bangle at the bandit who had held her — Bijan — saying, "Here."

However, she had thrown the bracelet low and in the direction of the hand with the missing digits. More importantly, she had lobbed it just as the bandit reached the rear of the donkey.

As hoped, Bijan had failed to catch the bangle, which fell to the ground near the donkey's hind legs. As the man bent down to retrieve it, Mary smacked the donkey on the nose.

The ensuing kick from the pack animal had struck the bandit right in the center of his forehead with a sound like a rock being split open. His head snapping back, the man had immediately been knocked off his feet. Sailing backwards, he had landed with a resounding thud and simply lay there. Upon closer inspection, Mary had realized that his skull was split open, and she could see his brains.

Before the horror of what she was looking at could seep in, her attention was drawn in the direction of their campfire. There, she saw the skinny bandit, thunderously shrieking as he was engulfed by flames. He tried to run, but made it no more than a dozen steps before dropping to his knees and then, as his wailing ceased, falling forward.

Sounds of a struggle had then drawn Mary's gaze to Joseph, whom she saw struggling with the last of their assailants. Looking around for something she could use to help her husband, Mary had seen the thin bandit's dagger on the ground. (Apparently the man had dropped it after falling into the campfire.) Without wasting a moment (or contemplating what she was about to do), Mary had scooped up the dagger, stepped behind the man trying to kill her husband, and stabbed him in the back of the head.

THE CARPENTER

Chapter 39

They left the bodies of the bandits where they had fallen. Knowing the type of men they were, Joseph felt no sympathy for them nor any obligation to give them a decent burial. Instead, he and Mary hurriedly packed up their belongings (with the latter retrieving her bangle after dropping the bloody dagger) and resumed their journey.

Initially, they traveled in silence. During this time, Joseph wore a look of consternation that had Mary worried. She knew that her husband was a godly man, and not violent by nature. Their encounter with the bandits had seemingly disturbed him. Up until that point, while they'd had to take certain defensive actions, they hadn't been directly responsible for taking a human life. Needless to say, that was no longer true.

"Husband," Mary finally said, "if you are distraught over what happened with the men this morning, don't be. We did nothing wrong in defending ourselves. They were evil, and their sins caught up to them."

"Ha!" Joseph barked, amused. "If you think I agonize over what happened to those bandits, I can assure you that is not the case. I fully agree with your assessment."

"Then what has you concerned?"

Joseph gave her a sharp look, as if surprised that she was so discerning. Then he sighed. "What bothers me about the confrontation we had was not the outcome, but how it came about."

Mary frowned. "What do you mean?"

Joseph gave her a pensive look. "I'm charged with protecting you and the child you carry. However, this morning, it was *you* who saved *me*. It strikes me that maybe I'm not up to the task."

Laughing, Mary took his hand and kissed it. "Husband, you have done nothing *but* protect me from the moment we left Nazareth. The mass of my one act cannot tip the scales against the weight of your many. No one could do better."

Joseph blushed slightly at her words. "You are too kind with your praise. You will feel differently if I fail next time."

She gave him a frank stare. "If *you* fail to protect me, it means no one could have done so."

Smiling at her words, Joseph brought her hand up to his lips, kissing it as she had done his. It brought a smile to his wife's face — and made her heart flutter.

THE CARPENTER

Chapter 40

Mary's words did much to alleviate Joseph's mood, and before long they were talking animatedly. Mary was particularly interested in the rest of their journey.

"How much farther to Bethlehem?" she asked.

"A day or so," her husband stated. "Much depends on the weather. We will also have to pass through a desert region."

"And once we arrive at our destination?"

"As I mentioned, I have relatives in the city. In fact, I have an uncle who owns an inn. We will be welcome there."

Mary bit her lip, but said nothing. If Joseph's Bethlehem relatives were anything like those he had in Nazareth, she suspected that the reception they received would be less than warm.

"It will be fine," Joseph said reassuringly, as if reading her mind. "Trust me."

She gave him a smile and nodded. Given everything they had been through in just the past few days, she trusted her husband completely.

With her mind at ease (for now) regarding that particular topic, the time passed by swiftly. Before Mary knew it, early afternoon had come, and — with respect to their journey — they had reached the desert region her husband had mentioned.

Upon first viewing it, Mary had spent a moment staring. There was nothing but sand, dry and hot, as far as the eye could see. (Of course, she had seen sand before, but not this volume of it, with no water or other landscape feature in sight.)

"What's that?" she asked, pointing out across the desert to what appeared to be a billowing brown cloud in the distance.

"Sandstorm," her husband said. "With any luck, it won't reach this far, or we'll be long gone when it does."

"I've heard it said that a powerful sandstorm can strip the flesh from your bones."

Her husband shrugged. "That may be. They can certainly sting your skin, and essentially blind you to the point that you can't see your hand in front of your face."

Mary frowned. "That sounds almost as bad."

"Well, if you're concerned about it catching us, we can always wait it out, or go back the way we—"

The words froze in Joseph's throat. As he was speaking, he had casually glanced back in the direction they had come from and noticed movement in the distance. People.

More to the point, he saw sunlight reflect off what was seemingly someone's head. Or rather, their headdress. Their helmet.

The Roman legionaries were behind them. And closing fast.

THE CARPENTER

Chapter 41

The vexation Canius had felt at the mountain had only been slightly assuaged by decapitating the mine overseer. The man's greed, ineptitude, duplicity — however one wished to describe it — had ultimately resulted in the couple getting away, because it was abundantly clear that their quarry had been present for some time before Canius had been shown the way out of the mine.

In addition, the earthquake and rockslide had cost the decanus three more men. One had died practically in front of him, his head taken off as if he'd been executed. The other two Canius had felt rather than observed, but their demise was no less certain.

Finally, after the mine overseer's death, immediate pursuit had not been possible due to rocks and boulders continuing to randomly roll down the slopes. Even when that apparently ceased, the dust cloud that the rockslide had created seemed to persist well beyond the typical lifespan and range for such things, making travel down the mountainside (as well as the surrounding area) even more treacherous than normal given the reduced visibility and the cracks and gaps in the earth caused by the quake. All in all, Canius and his men had been temporarily stymied, and he'd found it maddening.

When they had finally been able to continue the chase, their quarry was well ahead of them. However, they had a general idea of the couple's location, and also knew specifically where they were headed.

As before, Canius and the remnants of his *contubernium* traveled without luxury of rest or sleep, solely intent on finding their prey. Still, it wasn't until the

161

following morning that they came across firm evidence that they were closing in on their targets: the bodies of three bandits at a recent campsite.

Canius couldn't explain how he knew, but there was no doubt in his mind that the couple they sought had killed the three men. Like the decanus during the first encounter at the barn, the robbers had probably underestimated their prospective victims, and it had cost them dearly. Canius had made the same mistake himself, but he would not do so again.

Spurred by the knowledge that their quarry was near — the bandits had not been dead long — Canius and his men had run even faster than before. By early afternoon, their efforts were rewarded when, in the distance, they caught sight of who they were looking for ahead of them.

THE CARPENTER

Chapter 42

It only took Joseph about an hour to realize that they were never going to outrun their pursuers. Even getting into the cart and spurring the donkey to run at top speed had only gained them a small amount of ground. As expected, the beast had eventually grown weary and slowed down, at which point no amount of yelling, threats, or cajoling could make it go faster. Needless to say, thanks to the animal's languid pace, the soldiers had begun closing the gap again.

Basically, the donkey was an ordinary beast, and subject to the limitations imposed on such creatures. When hungry, it needed to eat. When thirsty, it needed to drink. When tired, it needed to rest.

The legionaries, Joseph now realized, apparently had no such limitations. They were seemingly galvanized by an inner reservoir — something that allowed them to dispense with the necessities common men required. Something that sought the same goal they did: the death of Mary's unborn child (and probably that of Joseph and Mary as well).

Starting to feel desperate, Joseph mentally went through the available options (which were incredibly limited) as quickly as he could.

Outrunning the legionaries was clearly not possible. It had already been tried and was proving spectacularly unsuccessful.

Taking a stand was absurd. These were trained soldiers, experienced in the use of weapons and sporting armor. (More importantly, the evil that possessed them was plainly beyond his ability to fight.) Ergo, even if he'd had a weapon, Joseph didn't fancy himself able to take on this particular group of combat-hardened veterans.

The only remaining choice seemed to consist of trying to evade them. They somehow needed a means of eluding the soldiers, a way to confound their dogged pursuit.

A shift in the breeze caused a spout of sand to blow into Joseph's face, interrupting his thoughts. Glancing out across the desert, he saw the sandstorm Mary had noticed earlier. It had grown noticeably in size and was actually moving in their direction.

And just like that, he had the answer.

Turning the donkey, he began guiding them directly into the storm.

THE CARPENTER

Chapter 43

It was an audacious plan, to say the least, but very much in keeping with everything else they had done thus far. Moreover, it was probably the best of the options available to them.

Joseph felt a slight bit of relief that Mary didn't question his antics when he suddenly changed the direction in which they were headed. She seemed to intuitively understand what he was doing and why. Looking to their rear, it became obvious almost at once that their intentions had not gone unnoticed: the soldiers had changed direction as well.

Joseph turned his attention back to what lay ahead of them: the sandstorm. One of the things he noticed almost immediately was that it was even larger and more ferocious than he had initially estimated. In addition, it seemed to be headed right towards them with a speed Joseph wouldn't have thought possible. One moment it was looming in front of them, billowing out broadly; the next, it had engulfed them, howling even louder than the flood they'd experienced, and Joseph felt sand striking all the exposed areas of his skin like needle pricks.

Squinting and keeping his head down, Joseph guided them farther into the storm. (Or at least that was his intent. Truth be told, it was impossible to tell where they were going.)

"Joseph!" Mary blurted out, shouting to make herself heard over the tempest.

He turned to her and she merely pointed down into the cart. Joseph looked and saw what had her concerned. The interior of the cart was starting to fill with sand from the storm.

165

In short, in addition to having to brave the storm itself, they were also going to be tasked with regularly shoving sand out of the cart. (It was either that or allow it to become so heavy that it couldn't move.) Frankly speaking, it was more than Joseph thought they could take on at the moment — especially with a contingent of soldiers behind them.

Unsure of whether he was making the right decision, Joseph stopped the cart at the top of a small dune. He helped Mary out, and then began unloading all their belongings. Next he swatted the donkey's rear, to get it moving. As the beast began trudging away, Joseph hastily pulled out the one item he thought they needed: the tent.

Initially struggling to keep it from blowing away as he unfurled it, he opened it up enough for Mary to crawl inside. He then had her turn around so that her head was toward the tent opening, which Joseph positioned to face downhill on the dune. Next, with Mary's weight holding it down, he went about placing all their belongings inside the tent before crawling in himself. Like Mary, he turned around so that his head was towards the opening, and then settled in to wait.

THE CARPENTER

Chapter 44

The storm lasted hours, which — based on its size and strength — was about what Joseph had anticipated. His expectation was that it would dump enough sand on them to effectively cover the tent and hide them.

By having the opening face downhill, the odds of sand blowing into (and possibly filling) the tent were diminished. With that risk minimized, Joseph was able to keep the tent open to the outside just a tiny bit, thereby allowing them to maintain a supply of fresh air. (That said, he did have to extend a hand to clear away sand every now and then as it piled up.) In addition, having the opening face down the dune made it less likely that someone would discern their hiding place.

In short, his makeshift plan had seemingly proven credible. In truth, the only shortcoming was that he had not truly considered how a mass of sand of indeterminable weight would affect his wife in her condition. Mary, who had complained little (if at all) since their departure from Nazareth, had spent the bulk of the time on her side — thereby keeping the weight of any sand off the baby for the most part — and only occasionally expressing a need to shift position. Joseph had found her attitude laudable and said as much, causing his wife to blush.

After the storm ended, Joseph was faced with his next big decision: when to break cover. Needless to say, he had seen no sign of their pursuers, but he also hadn't heard anything. Of course, that meant nothing. During the storm, the soldiers could have been shouting a foot from their hiding place and he probably wouldn't have heard them. More to the point, they could be somewhere close by now, and it wasn't beyond legionaries to be stealthy and quiet when it suited their purposes.

Not willing to take a chance, Joseph decided to wait a short while and see what — if anything — would happen. With nothing to do and unwilling to risk speaking, he simply closed his eyes while he rubbed his temples, intending to keep them shut only a moment…

****

A hand placed over his mouth startled Joseph awake. For a moment, he had trouble understanding where he was, and then he remembered. Mary, withdrawing her hand, placed a finger to her lips to indicate silence.

Joseph nodded to show he understood, and then he heard it. Voices. A moment later, he *smelled* it — a stench so powerful it seemed to seep into and through the sand. He didn't need to be told what it all meant: the legionaries were nearby.

"—'s gone, Decanus," one of the soldiers was saying.

"Yes, I know that," came a terse response.

Joseph recognized the second voice as belonging to the soldier he'd met in Uri's barn — the decanus. Taking a chance, he peeked out the slit in the opening (which was almost covered by sand) and saw a foot sporting legionary footwear.

They're right next to us! he thought, trying to stay calm.

"But they're here somewhere," the decanus continued.

168

"Agreed," said a third voice, "but do you want to waste an eternity searching?"

There was an angry growl, seemingly from the decanus, who shouted, "Who leads here?!"

At the same time, there was a whispering sound like someone rubbing their hands together once, and the blade of a sword came slicing down from above, directly between Joseph and Mary. The latter, watching a small stream of sand that accompanied the sword into the tent, realized how close they'd come to getting run through and placed a hand to her mouth in horror.

There was what felt like a lengthy silence from the three soldiers, and for a moment Joseph feared that the sword-thrust might have somehow apprised the trio that something was amiss.

"Fine," the legionary leader finally said. "We go."

The sword — which had seemingly been thrust down in anger — was then wrenched up, allowing sand to pour in until Joseph reached up a hand and pinched the opening through which it entered. He then listened intently, but heard no more voices, and a short time later the stench receded.

Chapter 45

Mary and Joseph stayed hidden for at least another hour, at which point it was getting close to evening. Assuming it was safe at that juncture, Joseph crawled out and looked around. He observed nothing but featureless dunes for the most part, but experienced a small jot of satisfaction when he saw how well-concealed their hiding place had been. Even knowing it was there, he felt he would have had a hard time discerning it.

Telling Mary it was safe, he helped her out and then began clearing sand off the tent. Following that, he removed their belongings and packed the tent back up. A short time later, they were on their way.

****

They traveled far enough to get out of the desert region and a little beyond. By the time they stopped, night had fallen, and they had been traveling for at least an hour by torchlight. It was not Joseph's preference to trek through the dark, but he and Mary had simply had far too many close calls lately — particularly during the last day. He was ready to reach their destination, and he was sure that Mary was as well (although, again, she never complained).

The area where they halted for the night appeared to be a regularly-used campsite. There was a ring of scorched earth encircled by stones (obviously utilized for campfires) and a tree stump close by that was essentially a natural stool. They quickly got a fire going and had settled down to eat some soup that Mary had hastily made.

"We should arrive in Bethlehem tomorrow," Joseph said as they ate.

"I shall be glad," Mary intoned.

"As will I," Joseph added. "This trek has been…"

He trailed off, unsure of how to finish.

"I know," Mary declared sincerely. "It's been difficult."

"Don't misunderstand," Joseph insisted. "I don't regret anything I've done or feel put upon. It's just that it's so much more than I ever contemplated. It means that you — and especially this child — are far more important than I ever imagined. I worry that I'm not doing enough."

"You're doing *more* than enough. More than could ever have been expected."

"But obviously I need to do more."

Mary frowned. "In what way?"

Joseph shrugged. "Maybe stand guard throughout the night. That way we won't have the issue of bandits again."

Mary laughed. "I don't think the Almighty wants you exhausting yourself in that manner. Trust in Him to handle the bandits."

"But maybe that's why he sent me — to handle the bandits and such. Maybe I'm here to be a sentry."

Mary shook her head. "No, if a sentry were needed, the Almighty would send one. Since He didn't, I doubt that one is needed."

"In that case, maybe I'm just here to carry your belongings," he countered. "After all, you're in no condition to lug them around. Maybe I'm nothing more than a beast of burden."

Mary giggled. "No, we have a pack animal."

171

"*Had*," Joseph corrected. "Now, by your logic, the Almighty would send a sentry if we needed one. Likewise, since we no longer have our donkey, maybe that's because we already have something serving that purpose."

"Husband," Mary stated, "that is completely ridiculous. You are an absurdly foolish man."

She spoke in a stern tone and with a completely serious expression on her face. A moment later, they both burst into laughter.

It took Joseph a few moments to regain his composure, and at that point, still grinning, he scratched his chin. "I appreciate your humor, wife, but I'm still not so sure that isn't my purpose."

"So what would you like?" Mary asked. "Do you need a sign to convince you?"

"Well, it certainly wouldn't—"

Joseph cut his comment short as a noise suddenly sounded from the dark. There was something out there — something large — moving towards them.

"Stay here," he said softly to Mary. Reaching into their campfire, he grasped the unburned end of a small branch and drew it out. Using it as a torch, he then walked off in the direction of the sound.

Mary waited nervously, worried about what her husband might encounter in the dark. Based on their recent experiences, almost anything could be out there. Still, as she had just mentioned to her husband, she trusted in the Almighty to keep them from harm.

Although it seemed much longer, Joseph had only been absent a few moments when a raucous sound erupted from the area where he'd gone. It initially gave Mary a start, until she recognized what it was: Joseph laughing.

A moment later, he walked back into their camp, grinning broadly. When Mary saw what he had with him, she almost shrieked with joy and began laughing as well.

What Joseph had brought out of the dark was their donkey, still yoked to the cart.

"Okay, maybe I'm *not* just a pack animal," he declared with a chuckle.

Chapter 46

Mary and Joseph made it through the night unmolested. Getting up early the next day, they had a quick breakfast and were soon packed up and back on the road.

Despite being close to their destination, Joseph was more wary than ever before. He kept an eye out for trouble of any sort. Much to his surprise, they encountered none. The only thing they met was other travelers on the road to Bethlehem, something they had seen little of due to the circuitous route they had taken, among other things.

In the end, they reached the city late in the day, but none the worse for wear. It was immediately evident to Mary that Bethlehem was more populous than Nazareth. There were more people, more animals, more homes, more shops…

While Mary took in everything around them from the back of the cart, Joseph focused on the upcoming meeting with his uncle. They had not seen each other in a while, but they had always gotten along well. He didn't know what, if any, tales his Uncle Benzi might have heard regarding Mary, but — unlike his father Jacob — Joseph was convinced that his uncle would not be discourteous or disrespectful to his wife.

In almost no time, Joseph found that they were at his uncle's inn. (In fact, he had been so lost in thought that he had almost bypassed the building.) He brought them close to the front door, then spent a moment dusting himself off before turning to Mary.

"Stay here," he instructed her. "I should be back momentarily."

THE CARPENTER

"Of course, husband," Mary replied.
Joseph gave her a smile and then went inside.

THE CARPENTER

Chapter 47

The interior of the inn was clean and well-lit, as Joseph knew it would be. His Uncle Benzi kept his place tidy and well-ordered; he disliked sloppiness.

The room Joseph found himself in was the hall, which was populated with tables and chairs, many of which were occupied. The patrons would be served food and drink here, and lodging would be offered upstairs. At the back was the kitchen, along with the personal rooms of his uncle, cousins, and other relatives.

Judging from the number of people present, his uncle appeared to have a thriving business. Of course, as Joseph knew, the number of patrons could vary substantially from one day to the next. As a result, business at the inn — as with most professions — had a tendency to ebb and flow rather than present itself as a constant and steady stream.

As Joseph stood watching, a young boy — maybe ten years old — came from the kitchen carrying two plates of food. He placed them before a man and woman seated at a table and then spent a brief moment talking to the customers. He nodded to the man and woman profusely, and then started heading back to the kitchen.

"Excuse me," Joseph said, getting the boy's attention. "I was hoping to speak with the owner."

"I'll fetch him for you," the boy said with a nod. As he left, Joseph briefly pondered whether he had just spoken with one of his cousins, although he was sure to find out soon enough.

He took a seat at a table in order to wait. Thankfully, he hadn't been sitting there long before his uncle came out from the back.

Benzi was slightly taller than average, with a lean frame that was just beginning to get a little round in the belly. He had a face that was generally friendly, framed by an iron-gray beard and matching hair.

Joseph rose to meet him, smiling and spreading his arms for an embrace.

"I'm sorry," his uncle said. "There's no room at the inn."

Chapter 48

Joseph frowned, somewhat taken aback. Had his uncle not recognized him? It had been awhile since they had last seen each other, but surely he hadn't changed that much.

"Uh," Joseph began, "I think perhaps—"

"No room," his Uncle Benzi said again, shaking his head in dismay.

That settled it. His uncle clearly didn't know who he was, although that seemed incredibly unlikely to Joseph. Uncle Benzi had always been sharp of mind and incredibly perceptive. Still, he was getting older…

"Perhaps I should try to explain," Joseph stated. "I'm your—"

"No need to explain," Benzi cut in. "I know what you're going to say, but it doesn't change the fact that we simply have no room."

"No, no, no." Joseph chuckled nervously. "I think there's been a mistake. I—"

"You want lodging," his uncle interjected, nodding. "Yes, I know. But as I keep repeating, we've got no room."

"I understand that," Joseph stated, "but I don't think—"

"I should probably clarify for you what I'm saying," his uncle interrupted. "We've got a number of travelers who've come here for some census. We've got foreigners from abroad who spend their nights staring at the stars. We've got Roman legions who've entered town just today, asking questions about new arrivals. With all of that, as I've said, we have no room."

Joseph stared at him for a moment, shaken by what he'd just heard.

"I-I understand," he stammered softly. "Thank you for explaining to me."

A moment later, he practically fled the inn.

Chapter 49

Upon seeing her husband's face as he left the building, Mary knew that something was gravely amiss.

"What is it?" she asked anxiously.

"There's no room at the inn," Joseph said, glancing around anxiously and reflecting on the conversation he'd just had. Benzi, plainly unsure of who might have been watching or listening, had been trying to warn him.

"I don't understand," Mary muttered in confusion. "Did your uncle… Did he not want us here? Did he not want *me* here?"

There was a pained expression on her face as she asked the last question.

Joseph took her face in his hands. "No. That's not it at all."

"Then what?" she asked in agitation.

He looked at her in stony silence for a moment before answering. "The legionaries. They're here."

Mary's mouth almost fell open. While she spent a moment recovering, Joseph grabbed the reins of the donkey and began leading it away, nervously looking around the entire time. It was due to one such apprehensive glance that he noticed the boy — the one who had been serving food at the inn. He was at the rear of the building, anxiously motioning for Joseph to approach.

Unsure of what this meant, Joseph decided to trust his instincts, which told him to find out what the boy wanted. Decision made, he hastily led the donkey and cart to the rear of the inn.

As soon as he and Mary were close, the boy said in soft tones, "My father wanted me to give you this." He handed Joseph a bowl of fruit: dates, figs, and more.

"Your father?" Joseph muttered as he took the proffered fruit, then immediately realized that his earlier assessment was true: the boy was one of his cousins.

"Yes, and he also told me to give you a message," the boy went on. "My father says there's no room at the inn, but there's a nearby stable where you can rest and are unlikely to be disturbed."

"That sounds fine," Joseph said, eager to find shelter now that night was falling (as well as for other reasons).

THE CARPENTER

Chapter 50

The stable in question turned out to be a cave located near the top of a small hill. The entrance was not particularly wide, but inside the cavern was fairly expansive.

There was a large fire in the center of the chamber that provided a great deal of light. Pens built against the cave walls housed various animals, including cows, goats, and a full-grown bull. Having unyoked their donkey and brought it with them, Joseph placed it in one of the empty pens upon his cousin's assurance that it was okay.

The boy (whom they learned was named Abiah) then led them to a small area near a back wall that was filled with straw.

"This is where we usually place travelers when the inn is full," he explained. "If you place a blanket over the straw, it's almost as good as a bed and pillow."

"It's perfect," Mary assured him with a smile. "Tell your father that we're thankful for his hospitality."

"He told me to stay with you, to see if you needed anything."

"I'm sure we'll be fine," Mary said as she munched on some of the fruit they had received.

Abiah simply nodded at this, but did not leave. Instead, he asked them about the journey from Nazareth while Mary and Joseph made a meal of the dates and figs. Joseph did most of the talking, answering his cousin's questions in broad, generic terms rather than specifics.

Joseph was just giving an overview of their trip across the mountains when Mary suddenly gasped and put her hands to her stomach. Instantly, Joseph was at her side.

THE CARPENTER

She gave him a knowing smile. "It's time."

THE CARPENTER

Chapter 51

Much to Joseph's relief, it turned out to be a remarkably easy birth — which was a good thing, considering that the local midwife was unavailable. Joseph had sent Abiah to fetch the woman, only to have the boy return a short time later with the news that she was preoccupied.

"She's attending another birth," his cousin stated, making Joseph groan in frustration. Undeterred, he had sent his cousin back with specific instructions to stay until the woman was available and then bring her immediately.

With no one else at hand, Joseph ultimately found himself taking on the role of midwife. Fortunately, he had attended many births in his time — albeit of animals. Mary, on the other hand, while not a midwife, had been present when several of her sisters and cousins had given birth, so she knew what to do. With her own knowledge supplementing Joseph's animal husbandry, it wasn't long before Mary was holding the newborn — a beautiful baby boy — in her arms.

****

By the time Abiah arrived with the midwife, Mary had already given the child his first feeding. Still, the woman insisted on seeing the babe, so — while Mary rested — Joseph led her to a manger where they had laid the child, wrapped in swaddling clothing. The midwife made what Joseph would generously describe as a cursory inspection, pronounced the child fit, and — after checking on Mary and stating she was fine — took her leave.

THE CARPENTER

After the woman was gone, Joseph went to check on his wife again, who was resting on the bed of straw (where, incidentally, she'd also given birth).

"I'm fine," she insisted. "I feel like I could walk all the way back to Nazareth."

"A bold claim," her husband said. "We'll see if you feel the same when I'm riding in the cart and you're walking the donkey."

She laughed. "I'll feel just fine. Now, go get the baby. I want to see him again."

Joseph rushed to comply, and moments later, Mary was holding the child, with her husband seated on the ground next to her.

"He's beautiful," Joseph intoned. "Perfect. Worth everything we went through to get him here."

Mary was about to respond when a cough sounded near the cave entrance. Glancing in that direction, Joseph saw several men clad in strange garments. Suddenly alarmed, he came immediately to his feet, at the same time looking around for anything that could be used as a weapon.

"Please," said one of the men, speaking with a slight accent. "We mean you no harm."

Joseph froze and stared at the men. Something about the tone of the one who had spoken struck him as being sincere. Moreover, they had not moved from the cave entrance.

"May we enter?" asked another of the men, also speaking with an accent.

Still somewhat nervous, Joseph nodded, at which point the men came inside. He noted then that there were three of them, and they approached him with friendly smiles. They stopped when they were a few feet away.

"I am Balthasar," said the one who had first spoken, "and this is Gaspar and Melchior."

Joseph acknowledged the introductions with a nod, then asked, "What do you want?"

"We came to see the King of the Jews," Gaspar answered.

"The King of the Jews?" Joseph repeated, confused.

"The baby," Melchior explained.

Unsure of what was going on, Joseph glanced at Mary.

"It's okay," she said with a nod.

Taking this as permission, the three men approached, smiling happily.

THE CARPENTER

Chapter 52

The three strange visitors seemed in awe and wonder of the child. Much to Joseph's surprise, they not only seemed to kneel before the babe, but also produced presents for him — rich gifts, like gold and myrrh — well beyond anything that might have been expected. It all left Joseph feeling completely baffled. Seeing his confusion, Balthasar approached Joseph, leaving his companions fawning over the child.

"I suppose all of this must seem very strange to you," the foreigner said.

"That would be putting it mildly," Joseph responded. "I'm not sure what to make of any of it."

"Then allow me to explain, if I may," Balthasar said. "Simply put, there is a prophecy concerning the birth of one who will be King of the Jews. King of Kings, in fact. The baby your wife has given birth to would seem to be the fulfillment of that prophecy."

"But how did you even know where to find him?" Joseph asked. "Not even my wife and I would have predicted that he would be born here."

Balthasar gave him an odd look, then said, "Come with me."

He began heading towards the cave entrance without turning to see if Joseph was following. Once there, he stepped outside and looked up. Joseph (who was indeed right on his heels) did the same.

"There," Balthasar said, pointing up to a star shining brightly in the night sky, almost directly overhead. "That is how we knew where to find him."

Joseph frowned. "Are you saying the star told you where to find him? That you followed it here?"

Balthasar nodded. "Of course. Have you never noticed it?"

"I've not had an opportunity or inclination to enjoy the night sky of late," Joseph admitted. "Even if I had done so and had noted the star, I would not have divined its purpose."

"I see," Balthasar said, obviously contemplating.

They stood there quietly, with neither saying anything. The silence stretched, but never became uncomfortable. Finally, Joseph asked the question that had been on his mind since Balthasar first mentioned the prophecy.

"Are you here to take him away?" he asked.

Balthasar gave him a look of bewilderment. "Whom do you mean?"

"The child, of course. Have you come to take him with you?"

"Why would you think that?"

Joseph frowned, then let out a sigh. "He's obviously important, and you know far more about him than I do. Moreover, I can't protect him from all the dangers out there — all the things that want to harm him."

"You mean Herod?"

"King Herod?" Joseph muttered, confused. "What has he to do with this?"

Balthasar spent a moment detailing their encounter with the despot.

"But do not fear," he said. "Although Herod sent men to follow us, we misled them. Also, we have already decided that, despite our promise, we will tell him nothing about the child."

"Thank you," Joseph said, "but it was not Herod of whom I was speaking."

"Then what?" the magus asked, intently curious.

Joseph was silent for a moment, wondering how much he should tell this man. However, before he even knew he'd made the conscious decision to do so, he was telling Balthasar everything that had happened since the angel spoke to him.

****

"So you see," Joseph said as he concluded his tale, "this child needs someone who can protect it, someone who can keep it safe until it actually fulfills that prophecy you mentioned."

"And you don't think you're suitable?" Balthasar asked.

"Do you?" Joseph asked sincerely.

Balthasar seemed to reflect for a moment. "You've defeated armored soldiers with mud, armed bandits with a donkey, and a wild boar with a blanket. Frankly speaking, I can imagine no one better equipped to protect and care for this child — not to mention the fact that, of all men living, the Almighty chose you for this task."

"But you can give him knowledge and understanding, increase the length of his reach," Joseph insisted. "How likely is it that he will fulfill this prophecy you speak of as the son of a carpenter?"

"As evidenced by all the signs and portents that presaged his birth," Balthasar said, "this child will draw attention wherever he goes. Distance and upbringing will not matter in that regard."

189

"In addition," the foreigner continued, "we're not soldiers. We're academics. If protection is required, we can offer little personally. And finally, despite the honor it would bring, I would not be so arrogant as to assume that I would be a better choice to rear this child than one hand-picked by Heaven."

Joseph frowned, but didn't say anything.

"You remain unconvinced," Balthasar surmised.

Joseph merely shrugged in response.

"If you will allow me, then," Balthasar stated, "I will give you an example from your own history."

Joseph's brow wrinkled. "What do you mean?"

"Consider Moses, whom Pharaoh tried to kill at birth," Balthasar said. "The Almighty hid him in the house of his enemy, where he was brought up in wealth and comfort. By that same token, He could have put this child anywhere and allowed him to be reared safely, chosen any man to be his father. But He didn't. He chose *you*. That has to mean something, even if you don't yet realize or recognize it."

Joseph was about to respond when he noticed torches coming up the hill. Men were approaching. Unsure of their intentions, Joseph was on the verge of going back into the cave to protect Mary when Balthasar spoke.

"Wait," said the magus.

Skeptical of what was happening but trusting Balthasar, Joseph stood his ground. As the men drew closer, he realized with relief that they were shepherds.

"Is he here?" asked one of the shepherds. "The savior we were told of?"

THE CARPENTER

Chapter 53

The cave had gotten fairly crowded, fairly quickly. In addition to the three foreigners, there were now quite a few shepherds present.

As Joseph understood it, the shepherds were in the fields tending their flocks when a chorus of angels appeared. The heavenly messengers spoke of a savior being born and told the shepherds where to find him, and they had wasted no time in doing so.

Considering his own experience, Joseph had no reason to doubt the shepherds' tale. In fact, he struck up a friendly conversation with one of them, feeling a sense of camaraderie since their encounter with the angels was similar to his own.

"You'll want to be careful while staying in the cave here," said the shepherd, whose name was Coby.

"Why is that?" Joseph asked.

"I think they're all blocked off," Coby stated, "but some of the connecting corridors lead to drop-offs where you can fall and break a leg, or even die."

"Connecting corridors?" Joseph asked, clearly not understanding.

Coby pointed to a spot on the other side of the cave, where a man-sized rock appeared to rest against the side of the cave.

"Behind that rock there's a corridor that goes into an extensive number of underground chambers and caverns," the shepherd said. "There are a number of them in here."

Looking around, Joseph noted that he was right. There were several other such stones at seemingly random spots along the walls.

"When we first started using this place as a stable, we would lose animals down those passageways all the time," Coby stated. "Eventually, we put rocks over the entrances to keep animals out, but every now and then someone who stays here wants to go exploring. Sometimes we find them, sometimes we don't."

Based on what he'd heard, Joseph had absolutely no desire to enter any of the corridors mentioned. It seemed an unnecessary risk to him, and one which he had no desire to take. In fact, he was on the verge of making a comment to that effect when the animals in the stable all began simultaneously raising an incredible racket.

The bull began snorting madly and pawing the ground. A young calf began bleating almost painfully. Their donkey began braying insanely.

In short, every animal appeared to be in some state of distress. However, it only took Joseph a moment to discern the cause: the legionaries were approaching.

THE CARPENTER

Chapter 54

Canius felt good at the moment. He was finally going to capture the man and woman who had been eluding him for the past few days. In fact, the last time had been just the day before.

At the time, he had been utterly confident that they would catch the couple. He and his men had them in sight, and — even with a cart pulled by a pack animal — there was no way the couple could outrun them. And then they had done something entirely unexpected: they had veered directly into a monstrous sandstorm.

Not wanting to let their prey escape, the decanus and his men had followed. Sadly, it had been folly.

First, it had been nigh impossible to see anything in the sandstorm, so tracking visually was a lost cause. Next, he had lost another soldier on the dunes when the sand shifted under the feet of one of his men, such that the earth basically swallowed him whole.

In essence, he was now down to three men (including himself), but he had changed his tactics since the sandstorm: rather than try to run his quarry down, he'd just go where he knew they were headed — Bethlehem.

Once they got to the town, they had immediately made known to a few key individuals — innkeepers and such — who they were looking for. Unfortunately, that effort hadn't borne any fruit. That said, Canius and his men had sensed that their prey was nearby; they simply needed to be patient. And then, just a short time previously, they had gotten an exact indication of where to find the couple: a nearby cave. As with so much that had happened lately, they couldn't explain how they knew; they just knew.

And so they had converged on the cavern, intent now on no less than killing the couple they had been chasing and their child.

THE CARPENTER

Chapter 55

Joseph didn't really need to confirm the soldiers' presence, but he did it anyway, running to the cave entrance and peeking out. Once there, he saw the light of torches glinting off the body armor of three approaching men.

Joseph dashed back to the interior of the cave, thinking furiously about some strategy he could employ. Unfortunately, the din from the animals was deafening, making it impossible for him to focus. Mentally, he wished they would all just go away for a moment. And then it occurred to him that maybe they could.

He quickly explained to those present what was happening and what he needed done. A moment later, most of the shepherds were busy opening the doors to all the pens and shooing the animals out.

As he watched them, Joseph caught sight of one of the blocked-off corridors, which prompted another line of thought.

Pulling Coby aside, Joseph asked, "The interior caverns you mentioned earlier — who knows them best?"

Coby shrugged. "I guess I know them as well as anyone."

"Great!" Joseph exclaimed. "You're our guide." He then outlined what he wanted.

****

It took almost no effort to get everyone organized, although it probably helped when Joseph mentioned that Roman soldiers would be entering the cave in moments with swords drawn. (If it was an exaggeration on his part, it wasn't by much.)

Basically, all of the occupants in the cave (the human ones, anyway) lined up and began entering one of the interior caverns, which Coby had directed several of the other shepherds to unblock.

Coby (bearing a torch and acting as guide) took the lead, followed by Mary — who was holding the baby — and then everyone else. Joseph, intent on making sure no one was left behind, stationed himself at the rear. In fact, he was standing at the cavern opening when all of the animals became even more frantic. A moment later, the three soldiers entered the cave.

To Joseph, they appeared incredibly gaunt, like they hadn't eaten in weeks. Looking at the decanus, even the change in appearance from two days earlier (when Joseph had seen him on the mountain) to the present was startling. Whatever was energizing them was also eating them alive, it seemed.

All three appeared to notice Joseph at the same time and started marching towards him. However, their progress was impeded by the flux of animals, who were in a complete frenzy. Whatever was wrong with the soldiers, the animals clearly didn't like it. They kicked or bucked when the soldiers were near, as well as reared up, and occasionally charged.

On their part, the legionaries drew their swords and seemed to hack indiscriminately not only at whatever was in their path, but anything that came near them. This proved effective with animals like sheep and calves, but turned out to be an error with the bull.

When the soldiers came near it, one of them made the mistake of striking the bovine with the flat of his sword. Already crazed, the bull went completely mad at that point and charged at the legionary who had struck it. The man was seemingly so surprised that he just stood there, letting the bull gore him through the chest.

At that juncture, Joseph decided that he had seen enough and slipped into the interior cavern.

THE CARPENTER

Chapter 56

Joseph hadn't intended on becoming so engrossed in watching the soldiers cut a path through the animals. Unfortunately, it had happened, and as a result he found himself well behind the group. However, the primary purpose had been achieved: the soldiers had seen him enter the corridor and would be sure to follow.

Showing a bit of forethought, he had asked Coby for directions before they'd gone into the corridor. The shepherd had complied, but the specifics were too detailed for Joseph to remember. That said, he had a vague idea of the direction he needed to go. Thus, with a torch in hand, he set off.

As anticipated, the tunnel was dark, but also unexpectedly narrow. Keeping in mind what Coby had said about falling, Joseph spent what felt like an inordinate amount of time looking down.

Walking hurriedly, he thought he picked up the sound of voices. However, he was unable to determine if the speaker was friend or foe. Even worse, the acoustics inside the cavern made it impossible to ascertain what direction the sound came from.

Moving as swiftly as he dared, Joseph continued to glance around nervously — especially behind him. He hadn't seen them enter, but he had little doubt that the legionaries had followed him. This theory was seemingly proven correct a few moments later when, looking to his rear, he saw a couple of torches perhaps thirty feet behind him. More significantly, he observed the light they cast seemingly reflected off armor.

With pursuit so unexpectedly close behind, Joseph suddenly found himself dashing mindlessly through caverns and corridors, looking behind more often than ahead, and paying little heed to where he was going. Somewhere in his mind, he understood that his antics verged on panic, but he couldn't stop himself. His body seemed to have settled on its own goal, which was safety.

He almost paid the ultimate price for his recklessness when he tripped and fell. Shockingly, although everything from Joseph's chest down had landed on solid ground, everything above it — including his head — hit empty air. Suddenly alarmed, he scrambled backwards on his hands and knees.

It took a moment for his dread to subside, at which point he reached for the torch, which he had dropped when he fell. Still on his hands and knees, he inched forward, holding the torch out ahead of him. As he surmised, the path he was on appeared to end abruptly at a crevasse, so wide and deep that he couldn't see the other side or the bottom.

Joseph gulped, thinking how fortuitous his fall had been. Turning around, he spent a moment trying to determine what he had tripped over but could find nothing. In fact, the only thing worth noting was a small cavity near the floor of one wall.

He was still glancing around when voices unexpectedly reached his ears. Looking up, he saw a torch (and the reflective gleam of armor) coming his way. At the same time, a makeshift plan entered his brain.

Staying low, he swung back around and stretched out his hand, placing his torch right at the edge of the crevasse. He then crawled to the cavity he'd noted and backed into it. The opening was barely big enough for him to fit into (and it had little depth so he would be more exposed than he'd like), but it would have to do.

He'd barely settled into his hiding place when the legionaries entered that portion of the corridor. Of course, he'd known they were near even before he saw them due to the odor that accompanied them. Their black eyes and haggard countenances were even more ghastly by torchlight.

As they went by, Joseph held his breath, trying to remain completely motionless. This was the most hazardous part of his plan. All the soldiers had to do was look down, and they'd see Joseph huddled in the cavity.

Fortunately, the legionaries seemed to be focused solely on the torch he'd left at the edge of the crevasse. As the lead soldier bent down to pick it up, Joseph crawled quickly and quietly from his hiding spot. Then, steeling himself, he rushed forward and shoved the soldier at the rear as hard as he could.

There was a clatter of armor as the legionary Joseph had pushed slammed into his comrade. And then both men fell into the crevasse, howling.

THE CARPENTER

Chapter 57

After the men went over the edge, Joseph slumped to the floor. He hadn't really exerted much effort, but he felt exhausted by the ordeal.

However, not wanting to waste time (and eager to get away from the stink of the soldiers, which still lingered), he climbed to his feet and began heading back the way he had come.

Unfortunately, his torch had gone into the crevasse with the legionaries, so he had to make his way in darkness. It was slow going, and he had just realized that he — like others Coby had mentioned — could get lost in the caverns forever, when he saw a light ahead of him. Still wary despite the soldiers being gone, he was debating on what to do when he heard someone whispering his name.

It was Coby.

****

With the shepherd's help, getting out of the caverns was suddenly no great feat. During their walk to the exit, Coby explained how he had found Joseph.

"Your plan was a good one," Coby said. "Lead everyone into the interior caverns and get the soldiers to follow, then bring them all back out while leaving our pursuers lost inside."

"Thanks," Joseph said. He hadn't been sure it would work when he devised it. The primary concern had been whether the various corridors interconnected in some way. Coby had assured him that such was the case.

"However, I think you overlooked the part where you were supposed to come with us," the shepherd teased.

"I got distracted," Joseph admitted.

"You also got lucky," Coby stated. "After we left the caverns, I realized you weren't with us and went back to find you while everyone else left — in case more soldiers came. A few minutes later, I heard someone screaming and realized exactly where it was coming from, so I knew where to go. I'm just glad it wasn't you who went over the edge."

"Oddly enough, I'm happy about that as well," Joseph replied, causing them both to laugh.

A few moments later, they left the corridor and Joseph found himself back in the stable. Based on where he stood, he understood that the passage he had exited from was not the same one he'd entered. Of course, that had been the plan, but seeing the actual outcome was different than simply visualizing it.

Glancing around, he saw that not everyone had left; his wife was still there.

On her part, Mary's face lit up upon seeing him; with the baby still in her arms, she rushed over to give him a fierce hug.

"You're a terrible husband," she said mockingly. "Don't ever scare me like that again."

Joseph was about to make a humorous comment when an odd smell caused him to wrinkle his nose. Understanding dawned on him in an instant. Shoving Mary and the baby away, he spun around in horror just as one of the legionaries — the decanus — came charging from the passage he and Coby had just left. Sword already drawn, the soldier plunged the blade into Joseph's chest as Mary screamed in anguish.

Then he pulled the blade out and did it again.

THE CARPENTER

Chapter 58

As he ran Joseph through — twice — Canius finally felt his frustration easing somewhat. But it had been close, and he had now lost all his soldiers due to foolishly underestimating the man yet again.

It should not have taken this much effort. It should have been easy.

With his remaining legionaries, he'd had the couple trapped in the stable. However, he had been unaware of the connecting caverns, which provided an escape route of sorts. In addition, the release of the animals had slowed them. (More than slowed, in truth, considering that the bull killed one of his men.)

Then, of course, there had been the ruse inside the caverns. Although shoved into the chasm, Canius had managed to grip the edge as he went over. Luckily, the man had not thought to check on his handiwork; one peek over the edge, and he would have seen the decanus hanging on for dear life. (And a solid stomp on his fingers would have brought about his demise.)

After Joseph had left, Canius had pulled himself up and attempted to follow, a task that became rather easy when a second person showed up with a torch. After that, it was simple enough to follow the two of them to the exit.

And then, of course, he'd drawn his sword and rushed out into the cave.

Much to the surprise of Canius, Joseph was still on his feet after the second sword thrust, although blood was now spilling from his open mouth. However, as Canius prepared to pull the blade free again, he saw someone rushing at him, screaming what he assumed was a battle cry. It was the other man who had left the caverns with Joseph.

Canius punched the fellow solidly in the jaw as he drew near. The man dropped wordlessly to the ground, unconscious.

Something clawed at him, and Canius turned to find that Joseph had slumped to his knees, but — still defiant — had reached out and gripped the decanus's wrist.

Canius shook him off without effort. He then gripped the handle of his blade and, after placing a foot on Joseph's chest, wrenched out the blade. Joseph toppled over, breathing harshly and clearly near death. Canius ignored him and turned to the woman.

Still holding the baby, the woman, Mary, began backing away in horror as Canius advanced on her. With lips quivering and eyes welling with tears, she merely shook her head, pleading wordlessly for her life and that of her child.

The decanus was having none of it. He had endured too much. Suffered too much. Lost too much. Someone had to pay.

A moment later, the woman's back was to the wall. There was nowhere left to go, no further place to retreat.

Smiling maliciously, Canius raised his sword overhead for a killing strike — a double-strike, if he could slay the child with the same motion.

And then the baby opened its eyes and looked at him.

Chapter 59

Mary, completely terrified, stood with her back to the cave wall, practically gasping for air as she held her baby. In mere moments, she had gone from being a happy wife and mother to — quite likely — a widow, and would soon enough be deceased herself.

Unable to move, she watched in complete horror as the legionary raised his sword, not quite believing what was happening. Filled with dread at what would transpire next, she sent up a quick, fervent prayer to the Almighty. And then the soldier froze.

It seemed at first that he was toying with her, like a cat playing with a mouse it intends to devour. But after a few moments, she realized that something else was going on. Although it was difficult to tell because his eyes were completely black, the soldier appeared to be staring at her baby, mouth open, completely fixated. It was if he were in a trance.

Slowly, without taking his eyes off the child, the legionary lowered his sword. Then, he haltingly reached forward with his free hand, extending a finger towards the baby. Much to Mary's surprise, the baby — its arm somehow free of the swaddling — seemed to reach to reciprocate, raising a hand towards the soldier.

A moment later, their fingers touched, and the reaction was immediate: the legionary's eyes became normal again. Then they rolled back in his head and the man collapsed bonelessly to the floor.

THE CARPENTER

Chapter 60

Lying on the cave floor with his lifeblood pouring out, Joseph struggled to get up, but couldn't. All he could do was watch in dread as the legionary went after Mary and the baby, and he cursed himself for being unable to protect them.

And then, without warning, the soldier slumped to the floor. Joseph hadn't had a clear line of sight so he didn't see exactly what had happened, but he smiled as Mary came rushing to him, the baby in her arms.

"Joseph!" she screamed, dropping down beside him with tears streaming down her face. "Joseph!"

"It's okay," he mumbled. He knew his injuries were beyond grievous — beyond treatment. "The baby..."

"He's fine," Mary assured him, turning the baby to make sure Joseph saw his face.

Joseph weakly raised an arm. "Let me...hold him...one...last...time..."

Mary, wiping away her tears, nodded. Ignoring the blood, she slid over and put Joseph's head in her lap. Then she lay the baby on her husband's chest, with his head just under Joseph's chin, and gently put her husband's arms around the child.

Struggling to move his head, Joseph gave the baby a kiss on the forehead. As he did so, a sudden warmth spread throughout his body, filling him with joy and peace. He knew without doubt that Mary and the baby would be safe now. Secure in that knowledge, he closed his eyes and felt himself drifting away.

THE CARPENTER

Chapter 61

"I must admit to befuddlement," the physician said after examining Joseph. "I've seen men expire immediately from far less serious wounds. We should be standing over your grave as opposed to your bed. Your survival defies explanation."

"I suppose I have much to live for," Joseph said, smiling at his wife (who blushed at his comment).

They were in a guest chamber at his uncle's inn, with Joseph lying in bed while his wife sat on a chair in a corner, holding the baby. After learning of Joseph's wounds, Benzi had sent a litter to fetch him from the stable, and they had been at the inn since.

"That still does not clarify how you healed so fast," the physician continued. "It should have taken months — perhaps even a year — to recover from your injuries, but here you are, essentially whole, after merely three days. The Heavenly Father clearly favors you."

"That he does," Mary confirmed.

"Well, I can do no more for you," the physician declared. "Your body has healed far faster and better than anything I could have provided."

"Regardless, your services are appreciated," Joseph said.

The doctor acknowledged this with a nod, then departed. Once he was gone, Mary moved with the baby from the chair to the side of the bed, next to her husband.

Mary placed a hand on his chest, on one of the places where he'd been stabbed. There was barely a scar there now.

They hadn't talked of what had happened, after he'd been wounded — how he had healed. But there was no need. They both knew the cause — the baby — just as they knew it was the baby who had stopped the last legionary.

As to the decanus, there had been no sign of him since he collapsed. He had still been present, unconscious, when the litter had arrived for Joseph. But when men went back later to return the animals to their pens, he was gone. They found his armor and weapons in a pile against one of the cave walls, but there was no indication of what had become of the decanus himself. (Mary had thought they could find him by the odor that accompanied him, but was shocked to learn that no one else — not even Coby — had noticed it. Apparently it was a condition only she and Joseph could detect.)

"So," Mary began, "you are considered able-bodied once more."

"That is the opinion of the physician," her husband replied. "And you?"

She raised an eyebrow. "Me?"

"Yes, you," Joseph said, laughing. "You just had a baby."

Mary laughed. "I'm fine. Did you not hear the midwife? I'm ready to have more."

"More?" Joseph said, failing to hide his surprise.

"Of course," Mary declared. "I've always wanted a large family."

Then she leaned down and gave him a kiss on the lips.

THE CARPENTER

EPILOGUE

The Horde was again in agony. Worse, all its plans had come to naught. In less than a day, all of its schemes had unraveled.

Once the legionaries it possessed had arrived in this town, the Horde had focused all its energy on finding the child. Its ability to track it had greatly waned, but it knew the baby was somewhere in the vicinity.

And then it had sensed it — some overarching change in the fabric of existence, some new force coming into being, manifesting.

The woman had given birth. The child was born.

At the same time, a chorus of divine messengers had descended from Heaven, not only announcing the birth to a group of shepherds, but also telling where the child could be found!

Almost overcome with glee, the Horde had made the information known to the legionaries. (Clearly, the heavenly messengers did not know of the Horde or plainly underestimated its abilities, because — despite not being present — it had heard their pronouncement as clearly as if it had been one of the shepherds in the field.)

Once at the stable where the child had been born, however, the Horde was thwarted at every turn. It lost two of the possessed soldiers in quick succession, and then the last — despite the Horde screeching in his brain — had made eye contact with the child and then touched it.

The contact had sent indescribable and unspeakable pain surging through the Horde. Unbelievably, the agony was even worse than the Horde's first encounter with the couple, and had driven it forcefully and painfully out of the soldier.

Tortured and tormented, it had sought a place to hide, to recover. A place where none would look for it. Desperate, it settled on a child — another babe that had been born the same night.

THE CARPENTER

Now recovering from its wounds, the Horde found itself greatly diminished in power and ability. It had clearly overreached in trying to destroy the child, but that was because it had not truly understood the nature of its foe. Now it did, and next time it would be ready. And then, when the time was right, it would strike — perhaps once more with a legion of soldiers.

Yes, another legion. It would make another legion its goal.

Another legion.

Yes.

It would be Legion.

Yes.

Legion.

THE END

(P.S. GOD loves you.)

THE CARPENTER

Thank you for purchasing this book! If you enjoyed it, please feel free to leave a review on the site from which it was purchased.

Also, if you would like to be notified when I release new books, please subscribe to my mailing list via the following link: http://eepurl.com/gjAdw5

Finally, for those who may be interested, I have included my blog and Twitter info:

Blog: https://sawsatypicalblog.blogspot.com/

Twitter: @AuthorSAWilson

25033799R00130

Printed in Great Britain
by Amazon